Ruins *of* Change

J. R. Dwornik

Brain Lag

Ontario, Canada
http://www.brain-lag.com/

Brain Lag Publishing
Ontario, Canada
http://www.brain-lag.com/

Cover artwork by Catherine Fitzsimmons

Library and Archives Canada Cataloguing in Publication

Dwornik, J. R., 1978-
    Ruins of change / J. R. Dwornik.

Issued also in an electronic format.
ISBN 978-0-9866493-2-5

    I. Title.

PS8607.W67R85 2011   C813'.6   C2011-902725-9

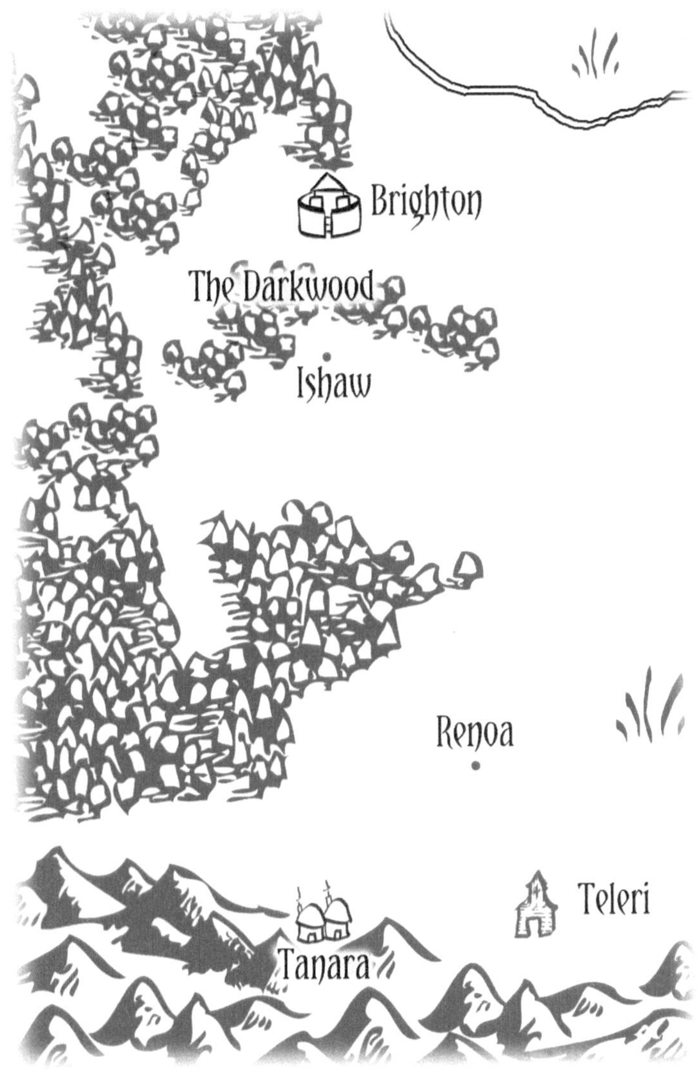

Brighton
The Darkwood
Ishaw
Renoa
Teleri
Tanara

Maia Desert
Lahn
Edan
Faneria
Orthys Mts.
Aura Lake
The Dragon's Teeth
Windygates Mts.
Unexplored lands

Chapter One

Kina stared at the unhappy pit that had appeared beneath her feet with wide-eyed fear. She hadn't expected the floor to give out, and she only barely managed to grab a collapsed pillar to prevent falling in after the ancient stones. She could hear the blocks break and shatter against the hard earth far below.

She focused her determination on the fallen torch, which illuminated the floor only a few feet away. She had survived much to reach this far, she would live to defeat this trap as well. It was her own slim, but strong, arms that pulled her out of the hole and back onto solid floor once more. She breathed heavily from both fear and exertion, and numerous scrapes burned her shins and forearms, but Kina Ukiel still breathed freely.

This pitfall was easy compared to her escape from the farmlands of Faneria. She had been young and naïve then, and never thought just staying alive would be a struggle on the streets. She fled the kingdom and survived royal knights, bands of thieves and horrible creatures. A simple hole in the floor would not do her in.

With a heavy sigh, she again peered into the abyss. The urge to throw herself into the pit vaguely pulled at her soul, but Kina refused to let go until her life was stolen from her final grasp. Letting herself die would be to surrender, to admit that she was not strong enough. Disturbed, she pulled her eyes away from the pit.

Gathering up her torch once more, she began to survey the passage with a little more care. The layers of cobwebs, dust and debris concealed an ancient temple. The complex stones that formed the floor had been supported by arrays of wooden timbers and stone pillars, but time had taken the wood and the mortar had long since eroded away. The entire temple had collapsed perhaps as much as a lifetime before Kina breathed in the cool airs for the first time.

Soon this place would be gone for all time. Roots from trees and other vegetation invaded the ceiling like long brown vines and slowly devoured the last passable tunnels. They would one day clog and collapse the temple completely, but that could be years in the future. There was plenty of time left for today.

Kina slipped her foot along the edge of the pit, seeking loose stones with her toes as she edged forward. Her goal was deeper inside and despite her solitude, she was not alone. Occasionally, she could hear the heavy feet of those who also hunted in the darkness. She could hear their curses and their screams. The life beneath the earth was not one that welcomed humans openly. The gods were claiming their sacrifices today.

Their voices grew soft as Kina continued forward. A few pebbles kicked free by her leather boots dropped within the hole only to hit the dark ground seconds later. The echoes traveled up to her ears as the only accompanying sound to her own breathing.

But this was her place, and despite her black mood, she enjoyed the challenges these ruins presented her. She enjoyed proving she could step above expectations and thrive where few dared venture. This was how she earned her living and she lived better now than she had as a child of Faneria. Windermere, a provincial town near Faneria's center, had been the home to her parents and theirs in turn. It was a place of gathering for people and surrounded by vast fields of fertile green lands. It was often visited by those of the royal house of Faneria, their standard flying high from atop the tallest point of the citadel. Though it was peaceful, Windermere had never been home to her.

Kina dressed well, her yellow shirt only slightly worn and more than a little dusty from her present excursion. Her pants were dyed brown, and coated again with a lighter layer of drying mud from her knees down. She had a vest to match, which sported only a few snags from her previous adventures. When her clothing was cleaned, she would not be mistaken for a villager. She would also not be mistaken for a noble lady for the choice of styles that could only be practical in Kina's world. A flimsy dress would be torn and ruined within minutes of entering such holes.

Drawing herself along the final distance around the hole at last, Kina scurried down the next corridor with short light steps on the uneven floor. She held the torch low so it would not blind her as she looked ahead for more signs of danger. Crumbling temples and unexpected roots were not the only dangers in such places. Sometimes traps lay in wait for the unwary. Worse still, there were creatures that claimed dark tunnels as home.

The tunnel she had chosen narrowed terribly ahead. The walls had collapsed in, leaving only a small hole large enough for a full-grown man to crawl. She moved carefully, keeping her right hand well in front to keep the burning torch clear of her face and hair. It did make it harder to see much further ahead through the glare of the flame and she needed to travel slowly through the confined space with the smell of burning pitch in her face.

She had learned her lessons well in youth. She had been navigating inside ruins such as these for much of the past seven years of her life. At first she had been forced into passages too narrow for grown men to navigate. She had hated these dark places then.

Soon, however, Kina discovered the signs of people living in these places long ago. Understanding and curiosity replaced anger and helplessness. After years of exploring collapsed corridors such as this, she had become less disposable to the band who had taken her in off the unforgiving streets. Now they needed her. They protected her from the cruel world, and in return she led them to riches unseen in several lifetimes.

Dim light glimmered ahead as the space expanded beyond the tiny cave she crawled through. Kina hastened to escape the enclosed space, anxious to stand once more. Scuffling forward, she exited and rose to her feet with a loud breath of relief.

That was followed by an even louder gasp; the treasure room indeed! When she had heard of this place she had dismissed the idea of a treasure room as a myth. The very thought of a place such as this being left untouched, with the population of Brighton so close, was mystifying. There were two small piles of golden coins and jewelry on an altar next to a stone pedestal and two tall, unlit candles. On the floor were numerous heavy chests, still sealed.

She didn't need any great intellect to decipher that this was an important place. These were offerings, gifts to whatever gods these beings had worshiped before they vanished. Large carved murals on the walls depicted a strange people in various acts of worship amidst the trees at the base of the temple. Often it seemed they cast great spells which summoned fascinating beings to do their bidding. Though they were foreign to her, they were oddly familiar at the same time. She had seen markings like these recently.

As Kina gazed at the ancient works on the wall, a flicker of light caught her eye and drew her attention to the back of the chamber. A deep rectangular box of stone sat alone in the darkness far away from the treasures that dominated the altar.

Tilting her head in curiosity, Kina approached slowly. There were no sources of light here outside her torch and the reflections off the polished gold surfaces. Without any treasures here, she wondered what had caused the reflection of light. More to the point, why was this part of the room neglected?

The unpolished surface of the stone looked oddly foreboding as she approached. It denied her the simple explanation that this place was a temple buried and forgotten. Such uncaring work flew in the face of the elegance of the rest of the chamber.

She leaned over the dark lip and illuminated the inside with her torch. A shape of a man loomed out of the darkness, and Kina shrieked at the skeletal remains inside.

"Fine," she declared to herself softly as she tried to calm her heart. She looked about the room and the murals and noted certain images no longer held any mystery. "Not a temple," she concluded and swallowed deeply. "Burial chamber." Judging from the images, a very important one too. The carvings showed dozens of people bowing to an object in a great ritual upon a massive temple, though she could now see that it was a casket.

Again she illuminated the skeleton, but this time she did so slowly so that she could study it. This was not the first body she had seen, and a skeleton was by far less gruesome than some bodies she had witnessed. In honesty, she found these far less torturous than the freshly deceased. It made them no less uncomfortable to see.

The body was covered by old material, long ago stolen of its original life much as the man who wore them. A dirty sword lay upon the chest with both thin, boney hands resting upon the hilt. A small, tarnished crown encircled the skull, resting unevenly around the head it no longer fit.

This place was indeed a burial chamber, and for somebody who once held great importance in this land. And much like the commoners of Windermere, he had died and was forgotten. The riches he had tried to take with him instead simply filled the forgotten room along with his fragile bones. All the power he once had was now meaningless as she, the lowest of all people, stood over his rotted corpse.

She whispered quiet prayers to Veran, the Goddess of Change. Though often maligned, Kina found it was always best to stay in Veran's favor. Those in power feared change, and those in need wished for it nightly. Yet change took all forms and favored few.

A strange object caught Kina's eye and she focused her attention on it in curiosity. The body had been buried wearing an odd amulet. It looked like it was made of glass, and was intricately carved with some strange writing, but it was no larger than the fingernail on her smallest finger. The way it reflected the firelight drew her eyes into it.

With her free hand, Kina reached in and delicately lifted it from the brittle bones. She avoided pulling, but the ancient leather necklace broke away despite her gentle touch. She hardly noticed.

"Okay, Your Highness," she muttered as she turned the object over in her hands and studied the bizarre markings, "why be buried with this of all things?"

A deep grinding sound of rock on rock stole her moment of thought and drew her eyes upwards. A stone statue of a man in armor, three times her own height, shifted and was now on the verge of toppling. Even as Kina watched the statue pitched forward and began to plunge downward towards her. She blinked once, hesitating in horror, before tossing herself aside.

Kina hit the ground hard. The torch she had been holding skidded away and went out amidst the suffocating dust. Coughing in the darkness, Kina lay still and waited for the rubble to settle. Cave-ins were part of the job, but she knew that was no natural event. She opened her eyes and could barely make out the crystal in front of her face. She choked down another cough and grabbed the amulet irritably. She would have to look at it later. She stuffed it into her belt pouch and clipped the leather bag closed.

The cavern was lit again by the light of a torch. Then two. A third joined in as Kina lay in the wrecked burial chamber. She recognized the voices and the appearances of the men who entered now. These were Drago's men, a nasty bunch of sell-swords. Unfortunately, Drago Kramoris wasn't leading them; instead it was a rough and sweaty looking man by the name of Loor who was in charge. Shorter in both stature and temper, Loor was not an impressive man. Thinning, sweaty hair plastered to his head and he wore a scowl that seemed a permanent feature.

"Gold!"

Kina looked to the coffin and nearly sobbed. The stone box had been dealt a direct hit by the falling statue. It had been split and crushed by the massive monument, spreading royal remains amongst the debris. Change was cruel to those fallen from favor.

With a heavy sigh, Kina sat up and regarded the mercenaries coldly. "Have you no respect for the dead?" Her question drew a few looks, though none looked at all chastised by her accusation.

"Do ya hear them complaining?" Loor asked darkly as he gazed about the room at the different treasures. Loor drew his sword and pointed it towards her. "And what've ya been doing down here, missy?"

Kina refused to be ordered around by Drago's men, even if they were more than a little intimidating. She stood slowly, ignoring the question long enough to brush some of the dust from herself before meeting Loor in the eye. "I promised I would find this place for Drago, did I not?" She tried to make her words sound more refined and impressive sounding to further distance herself from the likes of Loor.

"And I promised I would cut ya good if ya followed us down here," an unimpressed Loor responded archly.

A defiant smirk spread across Kina's features. "If I had followed you, I would be still lost in the darkness."

"Mind your manners." Loor unexpectedly charged forward and pulled his sword back in preparation for a vicious blow. Kina stumbled backwards and fell in a heap upon a pile of debris. She saw the sword begin to swing downward and she shrieked in fright.

The blow never landed, however. Kina opened her eyes to see Loor paused, looking over his shoulder back to the passage they had entered through. The rest of the men had parted and allowed Drago to walk inside.

"You lay a finger on her, Loor, and I'll have your bones spread from here to the Seas of Tremaine."

Kina smiled at her protector as he stared down at Loor. Even without his armor she could see him as a leader. He stood tall and firm amidst his men. His brown hair was nicely managed and his skin was clean. Next to his men he could have been royalty.

"Your thieving wench was about to make off with the treasure," Loor accused without backing down. Another scathing look with those piercing blue eyes and Loor did resheath his sword.

"I could not steal treasure like this even if I had intended to," Kina snapped back. "Do you believe I could carry even a portion out of this crypt myself?"

Her remark went unanswered as all attention was instead upon an angered Drago. "You promised me you could do better, Loor. Yet she is here before you again. Why is it you give me these empty words?"

Loor dropped to one knee and bowed his head. "Forgive me," he pleaded, hoping not to incur Drago's infamous temper. The smile on Kina's face grew slightly upon seeing the sell-sword fall into his proper place. Drago paid him little attention and instead approached where she lay in the dust. He alone loved her in this world. Not her parents who couldn't feed her, not her former lord who made her toil in the fields, only Drago Kramoris. He had found her and freed her from a life of servitude in order to help his band reach ancient treasures.

Kina raised her hand with confidence, smiling at Drago in anticipation of his help in standing. Instead he smacked her hand hard enough that the pain burned fiercely in her fingers and tingled in her palm.

"You were told to stay at the inn. I'll not have my men ignore my orders and I'll certainly not have the likes of you ignore me."

Kina blinked in shock, cupping her injured hand close to her chest. "I meant only to help you. I did not mean to displease you."

Drago was angry with her, and simple apologies never appeased him. "Be silent!" Kina pinched her lips together tightly at Drago's words. "I spared your life, wench, and that means your life belongs to me. Disobey me again and I swear it will be the last."

Drago moved on, ignoring her and gold alike. Kina sniffled, but maintained her composure and silence. He could not kill her. She needed Drago and he needed her. His band had not been so successful before she had accepted her role, but she would not risk further angering him. She had witnessed the madness of his temper and she would not be the subject of that wrath.

Drago stepped on one of the bones scattered across the tomb and deliberately pulled the dust covered sword from the grip of the dead king's ancient limb.

"This is why we're here," he proclaimed to his men, holding up the large thin-bladed weapon for all to see. Cheers rose with the men who celebrated their prize. Kina stayed silent as she was told but smiled defiantly. She had discovered the entrance to the caves and pointed the way, and she too was enjoying the moment of victory, even if she had momentarily fallen from favor.

"The Duke will pay well for that trinket," Loor cackled, looking to the men as though he had discovered it.

Drago grinned as much as his men as he cradled his treasure. "Gather up anything of value. I want this place stripped bare before nightfall."

"With pleasure," Loor answered. He leered at the treasures and Kina felt disgusted by the group of greedy men. Looting the tomb in such a manner felt as wrong as leaving the gold buried and forgotten. She knew the money would be spent on women and drink in various towns over the next few months. What remained would be spent on trivial items, which they would someday give away for favors in other towns. No joy would be spread to the people who served as slaves to their masters.

Drago noticed her. "Kina, you will return with me." His displeasure with her remained in his voice, but she could see excitement in his eyes. Despite his temper, she was pleased that he had requested her company.

She followed him through the tunnel his men had traveled, giving no further thought to his anger. She knew she was lucky to have his protection in this cruel world. Instead she devoted her time to the casual study of the traps the men had found. One never knew when such traps could be encountered again.

The tunnel was wider and clear of much of the debris than the path she had found. As she expected, however, it had been more dangerous because of this. Two of the men, nameless to her, were left where they died when they triggered a hail of arrows. Their blood seeped into the earth between the stones. She forced her eyes away from their ashen faces. She tried, failingly, to banish the thoughts of when she too would fall from Veran's favor.

Sunlight was a welcome change to the shadows and cobwebs. The vibrant colors of the surface world were filled with greens and blues. Within sight of the caverns was the great castle of Brighton. A small guard of horseback riders raced along one of the dusty roads bearing the colors of Edan's southern-most province of Deverell. Farmers gave them little attention as they worked their fields in the hot sun. The temple was a mere mound of collapsed debris now and the entrance a forbidding looking hole in the ground amidst a small cluster of trees.

There were horses tied near, but Drago had not given her one to ride. Instead she walked alongside as he rode. Kina was long used to such treatment. Horses cost money and often there was little enough to go around after the initial celebrations. She didn't mind as it gave her time to reflect upon her experiences once more.

How many centuries had passed since the forgotten king had died? What had this land looked like then? The fields of green farms dominated the landscape of the region. Trees were few and distant between, but she had seen the roots within the temple. Once there were trees here and the land had been much different. She closed her eyes as she walked and imagined the forests that had once surrounded the temple and the town that had been here before.

As they approached the castle gates, Kina once more marveled at the stunning size of the city walls. The wall was built from massive stone blocks, carved and carried to this location. It had taken years to construct these walls, and Kina didn't doubt that many of the workers died so that a long dead king had one more fortification to his name.

And despite the walls, Brighton was typical of every city she had visited before. People crowded into the dirty streets and a certain stench hung off those that lived in them. Peddlers swindled their customers, and soldiers would shove the weak out of their path as they went along their way without purpose. The citizens of this 'fair land' would accept their feeble existence and pay the taxes that allowed their lord to feast in comfort.

Her simple life in Drago's little band of sell-swords may seem inhospitable to the people here, but she found their way of life just as alien. She looked down on those who stared at her whether they be peddlers or peasants. She wondered which oddity they found unusual about her. Was it her clothing, which was so unusual for a woman? Or perhaps her short ginger-colored hair, a rare color in this region, matched only by an unlady-like style? Was it the powerful company she had in Drago Kramoris that drew their looks? Or perhaps it was her freedom they found so compelling.

"Does Brighton make you uncomfortable?" Drago's question caught her by surprise. She peered up into his blue eyes and once more marveled at their depths. Uncertain of her words, she found herself only nodding silently.

He laughed in amusement. "Relax Kina," Drago told her. "We shall leave this place behind us soon." He swung his bag off his horse and Kina snatched it as it bounced into her chest. It felt heavy, and the shape of the object inside told her it was the sword he had claimed from the crypt.

"Take this up to the room with you and do not let it from your sight. Brighton is rife with thieves." Mirth slipped away and was replaced once more by the seriousness that suggested that she do so without argument. "And have the keeper prepare you a bath. We shall dine with nobility tonight."

Kina blinked in surprise as she clung to the bag as though her life depended on it. "As you wish," she responded mechanically. Drago's horse picked up the pace and Kina stopped and watched him go. His dark blue clothes stood out among the townsfolk nearly as much as her own, so she was able to watch him for quite some time before he disappeared amidst the crowd.

She made her way inside the inn and did as she was told. In the privacy of her room, Kina allowed herself to relax. Her traveling bags lay next to the bed where she had left them and showed no signs of being disturbed. Content that everything was as she had left it, she began to unload her tools on the foot of the bed. Her dagger, while not fanciful, was a gift from Drago and served her well. She lay it next to Drago's bag. Her pouches contained the few coins that represented her own personal wealth. She frowned as she rediscovered the crystal in another of her pouches.

She looked at the odd inscriptions and found them unlike anything she had seen within the caves. If it was writing, it predated the burial chamber, much like the writing in the chamber predated the writing of today. While she could read none of it, she did have the stylized lettering well memorized.

The door opened with a creak and Kina instinctively let her right hand fall to the dagger on the bed. A small, raven-haired girl entered with a bucket filled with steaming water. "I'm sorry if I am intruding," she said nervously as she tried not to look at Kina. "I'm here to prepare your bath."

Kina smiled gently and brought her hand away from the dagger, knowing that the weapon was concealed from the door. "Thank you," she responded and not knowing what more to say, she returned to studying the crystal. Light refracted within, creating colors and flashes that drew her eyes within its structure. If a dead king had chosen this of all things to wear around his neck when he was to be buried, then it would hold great importance to him. Alas, without being able to read the inscriptions, she doubted that she could decipher what purpose it had held.

"Excuse me, your bath is ready," the serving girl interrupted again.

Kina turned and faced the raven-haired girl and gave her full attention for the first time. How long had she been studying that crystal? The tub was now full and gentle trails of steam rose from its waters. She noticed the girl was pale and appeared frightened, much as she herself had been at that age. She had not been much older when Drago rescued her from her dreary life in Faneria.

"I was once a serving girl like yourself. You have nothing to fear of me," Kina told her, though the girl did not seem at all relieved to hear the words.

"If you say so, miss. Would you like for me to wash your clothes while you bathe?"

Kina considered it only briefly. She was unused to being served, but at the same time she knew time would be short. If she were indeed meeting with nobility this night, then it would be best if she spent the extra coin to wear something unmuddied. She dropped the crystal back into her pouch and left it on the bed near her dagger and sought more usable currency from her change purse.

"I would very much like that. And if you could," Kina said uncertainly, "could you find me a leather boot lace I can use for a necklace?"

"As you wish," the girl answered. "Do you wish for me to come back for your laundry?"

Kina shook her head. "No, it's okay. I'll bathe now. How much does all this cost?"

"Not much for someone like yourself, I assure you," the girl answered quickly. "Only two Gulls."

Kina paused unbuckling her belt and looked over her shoulder at the serving girl. Two of the silver coins called Gulls this kingdom minted wasn't much, if she was a lord or favored knight. Still, tonight Kina would have a lot of money. She removed two of the silver coins from her small purse and looked at the crude likeness to the late King of Edan. It had been eight years since the passing of the king, and with no strong heirs to the throne Edan had fallen into chaos. Many of the nobility had become warlords in their attempts to claim the crown. She gathered up a copper coin as well before sealing the small pouch and letting it drop to the floor. Kina winced as she noted it didn't sound much like metal on metal as it hit. She hoped Loor wouldn't cut into her share of the treasure again.

Handing over the coins and her roughly folded vest, the serving girl seemed more interested by the mud that flaked off her shirt and dropped to the floor than the added tip to the fee. "What do you do, if you don't mind me asking?" There was a bit of a tremor in her voice as if she had ventured too far with her curiosity.

Kina tried to relax her with a friendly smile. She removed her shirt and handed it to the girl as she walked past to the waiting water. "I find treasures."

"Treasures? Where?" The girl seemed awed by the quick answer and her eyes lit up with excitement. Rather pleased the girl showed interest, Kina tried to open up a bit more of a conversation.

"Here and there. Even here in Brighton. Civilizations long gone once lived in these very lands. Their riches are often left forgotten." Kina folded her pants over her arms and thought about the race that had built the temple before those of Edan expanded to the region. "When a people move on, they can't take everything with them. So people like me travel great distances to find what was left behind."

"It sounds terribly frightening."

Kina's eyes snapped fully open. "Frightening?"

"Being outside the safety of the town walls makes me very afraid. The Darkwood forests are not more than a day's walk. There are creatures there that venture out and steal away the unwary."

A small sound of mirth escaped Kina's lips as she thought of the safety provided by such walls. She had seen those walls close up and knew that they were little protection against a resolute force. She nearly said as much when she recalled her walk along the wall. She had seen unusual writing scribed onto the stone blocks. Kina pictured a corner of the wall in her mind and realized that they shared many of the same stylings of that in the cave.

Suddenly, Kina didn't feel much like bathing. "On second thought," she said distantly, "just knock the mud from those and return as soon as you can. I won't be long."

The serving girl looked disappointed, but knew when she had been dismissed. She fled with the clothing as Kina lowered herself into the tub impatiently. Ironically, this bath was one of the few times Drago permitted such extravagance and Kina found herself wanting to be done with it. She settled herself by trying to focus her memories upon the cave and the strange markings within. She had heard of a people with long ears in tales told around mugs of ale. Stories of a race of magicians and secrets that vanished long ago. Just enough adventurers spoke of sightings to keep the old stories alive. Kina herself had listened to a scarred old man tell of seeing one as a child.

She doused her hair with water and ran her fingers through to prevent tangles. Drago sought power through riches, and Kina was determined to help him, but like today, she couldn't help but feel a strange compulsion to explore the ruins. When she was alone, walking where few had ventured in a lifetime, she felt powerful. An illusion of course, she reasoned. There were so many dangers that she couldn't let herself believe for a moment that she was strong enough without Drago.

By the time the serving girl returned with the dusty but no longer mud-caked clothing, Kina was nearly dry and pulling her gear together. There was no conversation this time as Kina accepted her clothing. She had her shirt on before she realized the girl was holding out a length of leather string. Kina offered her thanks and immediately measured it by eye quickly. It was a bit longer than she had hoped, but a quick cut with her dagger and it was well enough. The crystal weighed against her chest in a cool and oddly reassuring manner. She tucked it inside her shirt to hide it from view.

She slipped Drago's prized sword deep within her travel sack, though the wrapped hilt poked free of her bag by several hand spans. So anxious to leave, she nearly forgot her dagger where it lay on the bed. Though Kina had few real belongings, she felt great desire to keep close the little she did hold claim to. With the dagger slipped safely away on her belt, Kina left the room and the inn for the last time.

The streets of the old city were well worn and populated with many peddlers and townsfolk. Many more were soldiers of the Duke of Deverell. The people still looked to her with discomforting intensity. The soldiers leered at her and made comments toward her attire, the peddlers attempted to woo her with jewels and flowers. The worst were the scowls by the common folk who merely looked on as she passed. Their fear and dislike of her made her uncomfortable. Every town was the same. The common folk looked at her like a criminal, never hesitating to step aside but ever watchful of her.

Kina was quick to slip away from the main streets and into the shadows of the city wall. She recalled that she had first sought the shadows to escape for awhile and that she had come across the strange markings by accident. At the time she had found the peculiar writing interesting, but she hadn't recognized that it was another language entirely. If her memory was correct, and she had little reason to doubt it, then these symbols and writings were the same as those found inside the ruin.

Now Kina wondered if she had not found some connection to the ruins here in the city. She looked at the great block of gray stone and marveled at its size. It must have taken many strong backs to lift such a block for any length of time. The city was encircled by thousands of such blocks, but she reasoned few would be marked as such. This stone, however, had the round-shaped letters, and they were the same as those in the burial chamber, though worn by ages. She had no idea as to what it may read, and she doubted that she could find somebody who could read the strange letters, even if she searched the city for weeks. The letters became less distinct around the edges of the block and were not continued on the next stone, but she could see other blocks with similar markings placed randomly within the wall.

For a short time Kina wondered if the wall had stood in the time that the temple towered over the land. It was quite the image she portrayed in her mind, but her imagined city never existed as such. A more probable solution instead replayed as it had in other cities she had visited with Drago. As one city was destroyed, another would be built in its place. No materials would be wasted and much was reused. The temple was likely pulled down stone by stone to build the great wall lifetimes ago.

The temple then would be very old, predating the settlement of this region of Edan. Kina felt the deeply scored letters with her fingers and imagined what the land could have looked like then. These stones would have been squared and the letters finely chiseled. Now they lay open to the elements, slowly decaying over generations. Yet generations had come and gone and even the people who lived in this land had changed, but the ancient temple stones remained as a silent monument. In stories told, the Goddess Veran treasured nature and Kina could not help but agree with the old tales. These stones had held their secrets for generations. Even long after the letters finally faded, the stones would remain.

Chapter Two

It was evening by the time Kina quietly slipped into the waiting seat next to Drago. Far from her imagined settings, Drago's dinner with nobility proved to be in the same tavern they had been frequenting through the entire stay in Brighton. The place was lit by torches and oil lamps, which cast a warm glow over the tables. Dirty men fresh from working the fields and countless other common jobs drank merrily. Several women dressed in garish clothing whisked empty mugs from tables and replaced them with full, all the while laughing at their vulgar jokes.

Quieter men lurked where the light failed to penetrate, and Kina noted that some of Drago's men were tensed and ready for a fight. There were dangers here to the unwary, much like any she would find in the caves.

"Keep the sword out of sight," Drago ordered in a hushed tone to her. "Give no hint that you carry treasure."

She merely nodded in answer. In places like this she had long ago learned not to let on that one had anything of value. She had been robbed twice in such establishments, and threatened at the point of a knife in another. As Drago had explained to her, the atmosphere mirrored that of the wild. Predators hunted for easy prey.

Loor walked past the table, slowly, and spoke in a low voice.

"He comes." Drago grinned in a way that suggested he was pleased. She had not met their employer yet, but she recognized that he was a powerful person. Whether or not he was truly nobility was yet to be seen, but she had no reason to doubt Drago's words.

"Be watchful," Drago told her. It was a warning that she need not be reminded of.

The door opened and a wave of uneasiness started with those nearest the door that spread over the entirety of the tavern. The laughter faded. A soldier stepped in, ducking low to prevent banging his head upon the doorway. He stepped to the side and watched the people within suspiciously. Another followed and stepped to the other side. Then a smaller, rounder figure entered the tavern with a smug look Kina had come to recognize as somebody with untested power.

This man she didn't recognize but knew to be Drago's mysterious 'nobility'. As he walked toward her, she took in his greasy features and his confident gait. Here was a man who had not missed a meal, she thought to herself darkly. He dwelled in his own comforts, growing large, while leaving the work to those he felt beneath him. She doubted the sword at his side had ever been drawn but perhaps for show. She also noted that a number of the other patrons stood noisily and walked out, leaving drinks unfinished where they sat. This man was not well liked within Brighton.

"Ahh, Drago Kramoris! At last!" The man's voice was a deep baritone, but had a raspy edge.

Drago nodded deeply, a rare form of respect from him. "A fine city you have, your lordship." Kina sniffed indignantly, but her opinion of their greetings was ignored. She did take notice that the man did not correct Drago's lapse in protocol in addressing nobility.

"We of Brighton do take a certain pride in what we do," the big man returned with feigned interest. "Word has reached me that you have found the temple."

Drago nodded. "Found the temple, and the treasures within. The legends appear to be truth, so far as the existence of the sword goes." Kina wondered curiously what these legends were. She'd not heard of any that spoke of the sword or temple. Clearly Loor had convinced Drago to keep important clues from her in his failed attempt to plunder the burial chamber first.

"At last, the sword is mine."

Drago shifted, and Kina noted that his mood darkened. "The deal was we would be paid for our services." The big man shrugged. With a simple, casual toss he flung a good sized change purse on the table that landed heavily.

"Take what you want. Now, show me you have the sword."

Drago smirked. "Forgive me if I don't trust you, Lord Gawthrain, but your reputation travels almost as far as your name in these parts." Drago adjusted the purse to look inside at the coins within. Gawthrain scowled in response, but Drago had eyes only for gold. "Kina, show the Duke the sword."

Kina nodded and unwrapped the sword within her bag. She also took the meaning of Drago's words seriously. She lifted the sword in her hands so that Gawthrain could view the blade, but remained just out of reach of his chubby arms.

The Duke glanced at the sword longingly and shot Drago another angered glare before his eyes settled on the blade once more. "I assure you that all is paid for," Gawthrain growled.

"Perhaps," Drago remarked. "But a deal must be seen through. I want to be sure that none of the coins have fallen from your purse before you brought it here."

Kina allowed her own eyes to slide down the length of the sword. She hadn't much time to study it when she was investigating the tomb. She hadn't imagined that there would be anything special about the sword then, but there was apparently something of value to it. While old, the blade still seemed sharp and untarnished by age. Even the leather-wrapped hilt was intact. As she turned the sword over in her hands, she noted a circular indentation within the base of the blade that suggested something was missing. The shape and size drew Kina's mind back to the only item she had brought back from the caves herself. The amulet looked like a perfect match for the missing artifact.

"You forget your place, mercenary." Kina looked up and observed the Duke's flushed face. The two men were well focused on each other now, and it appeared they would be for a moment. It gave Kina time to satisfy her curiosity. The sword left on the table, she removed her amulet and compared it to the opening carefully, confirming in her mind that the two were once one. It wouldn't fit with the string she had tied through the hole, so she untied the strap. Taking the sword once more in her hands, she pushed the amulet into the opening. It was a snug fit and it gave slowly to her applied pressure. It sank into the final depths and came to rest perfectly aligned with the rest of the sword, giving a finished look to the blade. She smiled at her success and turned the sword over in her hands to inspect the fit from other angles. She shifted in her chair, finding that she was no longer comfortable with the way it pressed against her back. It was an unusual feeling and she looked up away from the sword as she considered where the sensation was coming from. It seemed to be from outside her body.

"Kina," Drago growled loudly, interrupting her thoughts. She looked up and met his eyes and saw only rage within. She shrank away from him slowly, bringing the sword close to her.

"What is that?" the Duke snarled. He was already standing with his sword pointing at her, though he had stepped back and looked frightened.

Fear was fast flooding into her body now as she realized that once more she appeared to be in trouble. Only this time she had no idea what trap she had stepped into. Drago was drawing his own sword, backing out of his chair in the same motion so that he could stand. She noted that the building had grown quiet but for whispers and moving chairs. Eyes turned to her and weapons were drawn.

"What did I do?" she whimpered to Drago, hoping for forgiveness.

"What evil magic is this?" Gawthrain demanded. Almost as one, both the Duke and Drago moved in on her, swords swinging. Kina leaned back and fell from her chair, kicking it out into Drago's knees and knocking him back. With the table between her and the Duke, Kina rolled to her feet.

"I'm sorry," she cried, backing away from the angry men. They moved around the obstacles and continued to approach her slowly. Sounds around her told her she was fast running out of room to move. Others were closing in on her now. By sound alone she heard a large man swing at her. Instinct drove her, she ducked low and the sword whistled over her head. She raised her arms and the sword in her hands deflected the return blow. The strength of it still threw her on her back again.

"Get her!" She had no idea who yelled it, but the entire tavern came to life with angry sounds in response. Kina rolled to her feet and ran for the door as fast as she could. Men tried to stop her, they stood in front of her and swung swords, clubs and even their own fists as they came within reach. She ducked and dodged, dancing around each in turn. Even the smallest opening between them she exploited, sometimes passing between sharpened blades by the width of her fingertips. Kina was no fighter and she was not known to be particularly nimble. How she knew where they were she did not know, but it seemed to her that she was hearing the attacks with just enough time to react.

The door was closed, but Kina braced herself, drawing her arms in and throwing her shoulder into the wooden door. It blew open and she tumbled to the ground outside. It was dark and the air was cool, but Kina didn't give herself a moment to rest. The men were after her still and she needed to find a place to hide. She paused as she put her hands on the ground, noticing now that she still held the sword in her hands. She caught her reflection in the polished steel, and while distorted, she noted features that she had not been born with. A set of sharp animal-like ears protruded through her hair like a beacon. She brought a hand to one, feeling contact both on her fingers and the ears.

"What're these?" she whispered, her voice trembling. She slid her hand down to where her own ears should have been and found nothing but smooth skin. "What happened to me?" she gasped, barely able to keep herself from tears.

She looked over her shoulder at the door, seeing the first of her pursuers pause as he looked at her. A tail interrupted her glance, a tail that seemed to be her own. Realization struck her and the man seemingly at the same time. Her eyes grew large, as did his. She shrieked. Later she would understand that she had been lucky. His hesitation had bought her precious moments to recover from shock and regain her feet. The man at the door was pulled aside as other, less hesitant men resumed the chase. Kina grabbed the sword tightly in her hands and ran with all her strength.

For the moment, it seemed her luck was holding. She passed several townsfolk as she ran, but always they stepped aside when they saw her come. Kina gritted her teeth as a soldier spotted her and flinched aside to let her pass. She was a freak now. An armed monster running free within the city. Tonight they would lock the doors for fear of what was to come. Deep inside she felt dark bitter laughter at the thought of the servant girl. She worried for what was outside the city walls, never realizing the woman she tended to would become a monster only hours later.

Quietly, she slipped into a stable and looked within for further danger. The horses paid her little mind, and the help had apparently finished up for the day. There were plenty of places to hide here, and with luck she would be able to remain safely hidden until morning. Things would be better in the morning, she thought helplessly. Drago would fix whatever had happened, and she would be welcomed back with that grin of his that he flashed her whenever she overreacted. Kina climbed up into the loft and plodded carefully over the loose hay. She had chosen worse spots to hide in her time, so the prospect of laying on the straw was not wholly unacceptable. She understood the value of need and necessity, and chose a spot where she could be both out of sight and yet could see the entrance. With the sword laying beside her in the hay, Kina watched the door anxiously. Aside from the noises from the horses, it seemed she had escaped.

Kina sighed and relaxed. She glared at the sword unhappily. Somehow it was to blame for all this. Through all the stories of magic, she had never heard of such a spell. Unfortunately, she knew admittedly little about what magic could do and had never witnessed real magic in her life. As ancient as it was, the blade was unblemished by chips or tarnish. Without the layer of dust it appeared freshly made. Her amulet had fit perfectly within the hilt of the sword, leaving her little doubt that it belonged there. By inserting the crystal, clearly she had unlocked some sort of ancient spell.

She drew her knife slowly as she stared at the sword, and wondered if taking the crystal back out would break the spell. She tried to wedge the blade of her knife into the edge and lever the crystal out. The blade just slipped over the narrow crack between crystal and sword. With growing frustration, Kina tried again. Each time she tried she found she was unable to get anything in deep enough to wedge the crystal out. She abandoned the knife and tried with her own fingernails, however she met with no success. Tired, and now with sore fingers, Kina abandoned her attempts.

She lifted the sword and gazed at the blade with wonder. Could it really be magical? It seemed farfetched to believe, but clearly something had changed within the tavern. It was also a sword that the Duke had shown interest in purchasing. In fact, he had seemed interested in the sword alone. Since it had obviously been undisturbed since the fall of whatever kingdom existed before Edan, Gawthrain had to have learned of the sword elsewhere. She needed to learn more. Somebody somewhere knew about this sword and would be able to tell her how it changed her and how it could change her back.

Kina set the sword down and curled up next to it. She gazed at the weapon tiredly as she got comfortable next to it. The weapon of a dead king, sought by the likes of the Duke of Deverell, and possibly an item of magic, and yet it seemed to her just another weapon of man. Kina yawned and closed her eyes. Tomorrow she would find Drago and everything would be better.

Kina awoke with uncertainty. Straw poked her through her clothing, and she shifted in the hay unhappily. Something seemed off to her. The sounds below were of horses, clomping on the wooden floor and breathing in snorts. She felt some straw poke her in an unusual place and she whirled noisily in reaction. She grabbed the tan-colored tail and brushed small bits of hay from the furry appendage. This was not a happy discovery. She was still a monster. And it *hurt* when straw poked her tail.

A noise stilled her motions and Kina listened carefully. Was somebody else present as well? Kina began to lean forward in the hay again so that she could peek over the edge at the floor below. Sudden movement close to her caused her to jump, and there was a loud call of triumph as a man leapt up the final steps of the ladder. There was weight on her, holding her down in the hay and hands fought to grab a hold of her wrists.

"Thought ya could escape, did ya?" Loor's voice grated. Kina's eyes sprung wide as she realized who her attacker was. There was no relief in her recognition. She fought even harder to break free, even as he successfully pinned one of her arms down in his strong grip. She searched frantically for anything that might be within reach of her other arm while trying to keep moving enough to prevent being completely pinned. "Thought ya could steal from us? I'll teach ya. I'll teach ya a lesson and then cut you up so that ya don't cause no more trouble for me."

"Let go," came her response, feeble even in her own ears. Loor wouldn't let her go. She needed to act for herself. She kicked at him, but he was positioned high enough on her that her attacks merely rocked them in the hay. Loor chuckled darkly at her, breathing into her face with foul breath, "I think I see why Drago likes ya so. You've got a lot of fight, don't ya girl?"

Glaring at Loor, Kina continued to struggle. Her free hand came in contact with something solid and she swung it with all her might. There was a look of surprise on Loor's face before he reacted. He tried to stop her swing, however her weapon bit deeply within his arm as he tried to block the blow. He yelped loudly and fell away from her, though she didn't feel his weight hit the hay. Instead there was the delayed thump of his body hitting the wood floor below. Kina panted heavily, shocked by what she had done. The blood on the sword trickled down the blade toward the hilt. She dropped the sword into the straw and scrambled to look over the side of the loft for Loor. He lay on his back staring upward with a strange, frightened look that remained unchanging. It took her only a moment to realize that he was no longer among the living, but she could still feel the intimidating presence he had over her.

She needed to escape, she realized. Drago would not be pleased with her at all for her hand in Loor's death. The sword's curse continued to haunt her. She looked at the bloodied blade and nearly left it where it lay. Had it not been the only link she could think of to her transformation, she probably would have left it. Kina wiped the blood off on the hay before packing the sword away the best she could in her bag. She tipped the bag back over her shoulder and began down the ladder.

Outside she could hear voices approaching. No doubt Loor had been heard and now folk were coming to investigate. Again she needed to run, but this time she would need to go further. She looked at the horses around her and decided her next course of action quickly. While she had rarely been on the big animals, she knew what they were capable of. She wouldn't be able to out distance experienced riders, but she would have a head start. She hoped that would be enough.

She picked a horse nearly at random, avoiding those still restless from the noise she had made with Loor. She only looked to see if it looked strong, but she had no way of knowing whether or not her choice was good at a glance. The first horse she saw looked big and intimidating, but she saw no reason not to take it. It was a brown creature, with longer black hair and tail. Kina opened the gate to the stall and took good care leading the horse from its enclosure. Once she had it out, however, she realized just how daunting a task stealing a horse would be. She couldn't begin to figure out how she would climb up on the great beast's back.

"Hey!" The young man's voice made her jump back in fright, but it wasn't an armed soldier. "What are you doing back there?"

Kina realized belatedly that the young man couldn't see her as well as she could see him. She remained mostly within the shadows inside the wooden structure and further hidden by the horse itself. She thought quickly, sizing up the man as she sought out a plan. He looked like he might be a simple stable hand, and he seemed too young for any full tradesman. He dressed simply, and his clothes looked near as worn as her own, so she banked her plan upon her quick observations.

"I am sorry, I need to ready my master's horse, but I cannot figure out how to get the saddle on." Kina backed up a stride to further hide herself from the boy, pretending to be shy and meek. It bought her a moment more to grab a blanket from a hook on the wall and toss it around her shoulders. It hid her tail, mostly, but her ears remained in the open.

"Is this your master's horse?" the man asked as he came inside. "I'm afraid this is very unusual, miss."

"I am sorry, but my master was in a hurry to leave." She wished she had a hat or something.

"Oh." The stable hand seemed to relax. He stepped inside with less apprehension and no longer appeared concerned by the invader. "If he is part of the hunting party, he should have waited for the Duke. He is arranging some kind of gathering this morning."

Kina flinched. "Um, yes. Well, my master insisted that I get his horse ready early. He is trying to catch the monster first. Something about wanting the reward himself." She became more aware of Loor's body laying just around the only hay stack on the ground level, full view for her but for the moment hidden to his young eyes.

"He should really wait. I'm going to have all the horses ready by then, so you do not have to worry about it."

"No," she answered firmly, probably more firmly than she should have. "No, my master was quite anxious." She thought quickly again. "Perhaps he would share the reward with you if you do this favor for me?"

The boy paused a moment, still clearly unable to see her well. He tried moving closer, but she continued to keep her distance. She gathered up her bag and moved along behind the horse.

"Look, I'll give you a hand. Which saddle is his?"

"Oh," she gasped with false enthusiasm. "Thank you, young master." She looked back the way the boy had come to a row of saddles away from Loor's body. "That one, right there, the black one. That one is my master's."

The stable hand turned and looked at the saddles before grinning at her. "That one? Okay, you hold that horse right there and I will saddle him up for you."

"Thank you, thank you again." She patted the horse hoping that it would be patient and forgive her for what she was doing. As the youth carried the heavy looking saddle back she realized she wasn't going to be able to hide much longer. She moved to the far side of the horse, and tossed away the blanket. It would be of no further use to her now.

The saddle flopped onto the back of the horse, and the youth began to tighten buckles. "A fine horse your master has. This one looks as though he could run from here to Faneria." Kina wasn't sure if he was exaggerating. It was an awful long way to the neighboring kingdom, but her knowledge of horses stole away any response she may have made.

"You certainly dress oddly, miss, if you don't mind me saying so."

She froze, but quickly forced herself to move lightly. "Are you stealing glances at me, young master?"

"Why do you try to hide yourself? You sound quite pretty," he answered, sounding somewhat embarrassed. Kina twitched, wanting to believe his words could be true. She had never been a beautiful woman, far too thin, as Drago's lot were fond of reminding her. What now would they think of her appearance? Loor's remarks were silenced, but she found no solace in that.

The boy tightened the straps on the bridle with a steady hand and practiced ease. It hardly distracted his young mind, and he continued to question her in interest. "You don't look like you spend much time in the city. What is it your master does?"

"I say, you are being quite forward. I might be insulted to hear such implications from your mouth."

"Apologies." The youth moved about the horse quickly, faster than she expected, but not faster than she was prepared for. She stood with dagger drawn fully unhindered or hidden by her bag. It was clear the stable hand wasn't expecting to come face to face with an armed opponent with strange ears after talking to some waif over a horse.

"Hold your tongue," she hissed as she pointed her dagger at him. She dropped the accent she had adopted and spoke in natural tones. "I mean you no harm."

Open mouthed, the youth nodded. He was quite handsome, barely coming into his manhood, she realized. If he were to try to fight her, she doubted she could beat him. Her appearance, however, had instilled a certain amount of respect for her, and she didn't want to lose the advantage to him.

"I only want the horse."

"You're the monster," he whispered, much to her annoyance. "From last night," he added quickly.

"I am. You will find I'm quite dangerous when angered, so please do as I say." She hoped her bluff would be enough to frighten him into silence. The youth gulped and nodded slowly.

"Is the horse ready?" Again a slow nod. "Good. Now step back."

She looked at the stirrups uncertainly, realizing it was a long step upwards for her to reach the loop with her foot. She looked at the youth again, and he backed away. Content, she slipped her dagger back into her belt and grabbed hold of the saddle. It wasn't a graceful climb, but she managed to gather herself in the saddle without frightening the horse.

"Pass me my bag," she ordered the stable hand. When she saw him hesitate she added, "I'll be gone once I have my pack. I want for nothing more than to put some distance between these walls and myself."

"Uh, right." He hurried over and did as she asked. He reached uncertainly for her, keeping his hands distanced from her as though she would take them and anything else that strayed too closely. She collected the bag gently to show that she wasn't entirely a monster, if perhaps only for herself.

"You don't really expect to get far, do you?" the youth asked. Kina glared at him before realizing that she heard no malice in his voice. "You don't know how to ride a horse."

"Then I need to depend on what help I can get," she answered firmly. "If you could delay in telling of my departure it would be appreciated, though I'll fully expect that others will tell of me." She leaned forward on the horse with little hope. "Veran," she whispered to the horse wistfully, "you have treated me unfairly. Please help me now. Please, let this beast run like the wind."

To her surprise, the horse made a loud whinny and reared its head back. She yelped and nearly fell off the saddle backwards as the horse sprang forward. She flailed for a moment before leaning down as low forward as she could get to the horse. It seemed safer to hold the horse with her own arms than to trust the leather saddle that the youth had placed upon it.

Buildings flashed by at frightening speed as the horse steered through the streets on its own accord. It was all she could do just to hold on. She could feel the wind in her hair and in her face. Tears streamed from her eyes and she squeezed them closed in fright.

"Rider comin'!" a voice called out. She opened her eyes and looked to the voice, a guard watching her anxiously from the wall. From his position, she wondered if he could tell that it was a monster fleeing the city. It seemed not, as ahead of her the gates opened and the doors parted. The soldiers seemed all too eager to help her escape. Then, she thought, they had no reason to believe she was anything but a citizen at this time. Veran, she thought, had indeed listened to her plea.

The soldiers had a moment to relax with their task completed, a moment in which they watched her come. In that moment, she realized she was close enough for them to see perhaps too clearly. There was a stunned look as she neared, and suddenly they were scrambling to close the gates again. She flashed by them before they had a chance to do much more than begin the task. Their angered cries ordered her to halt as she sped into the fields beyond the great walls.

"Thank you," she whispered to the horse. She looked back at the city of Brighton and smiled with her moment of triumph. It wasn't much, she knew, but she had escaped. At least now she had a chance to disappear. The horse slowed its pace to a trot but still seemed to cover more ground with each stride than she would have been able to. The beaten path in the ground that slid along beneath its hooves headed what seemed to her as south. It was difficult to tell for certain, being bounced about and holding on tightly, but she drew upon her knowledge of Brighton's walls and decided it was the south gate she had just escaped from. If that were true, it meant she was quickly heading for the ancient forest that stretched nearly to the borders of Faneria. An old wood where the locals would not follow her. The Darkwood.

Closing her eyes, Kina drew upon the memories of maps she had seen of this land. If accurate, the Darkwood wasn't as wide as it was long. Even by foot it shouldn't take more than a few hours to cross. At the speed at which the ground flashed by beneath her, Kina doubted she would have much time to be frightened of anything within the woods.

It was perhaps midday that Kina saw the trees rising over the ridge. The path strayed away from the trees and to a rocky, uneven hill heading east to Faneria. The beast tried to follow the path, but Kina reluctantly pulled on the reins. Her goal was clear, the horse must have known that, but it steadfast refused to move closer to the Darkwood. After a moment of silent disagreement, the horse made loud protests and slowed to a halt with little intention of bringing her closer. She frowned and tried to get the horse to continue with little success.

Kina looked back over the trail she had come and spotted the riders. She had hoped that some of her pursuers would have given up the chase, but there remained more than she could count. She could hear them already, the angry pounding of hooves on the hard earth, a low rumble of thunder, but they were still distant enough if she acted fast.

She considered her escape carefully now. She knew to stay on the path meant that Drago would eventually catch up and then her life would be forfeit. Alternatively, the Darkwood would take longer to cross on foot. Unfortunately, there was not much choice to be had. She had to venture into the woods. As she stared deeper between the trees into the shadows beyond, she felt some unnamed primal fear grip her heart. Something evil lived there.

It mattered little, the trees offered her best hope of escape. Once more, Kina tried to convince the horse to move forward into the trees. The restless beast would have none of it however, and stumbled back with a loud protest.

A sigh, and Kina slipped off the back of the horse. "Then this will be where we part," she whispered to the animal. She wished no ill upon the horse, but her escape would be further complicated by the loss in mobility. "Run free, and with speed," she ordered and then sent the horse running for the hills. She hoped it would distract the riders, but she held little expectation that such a simple trick would work.

The trees now were her focus. "None who have entered have ever returned," she muttered. "But perhaps those who have come before me also shared in my dislike of Brighton." Kina plunged into the old woods at a run.

These trees were not normal, Kina thought darkly as she ran between the tall trunks. The ground around offered little vegetation to hide within and the trees provided no low branches for which to climb. All the while an oppressive feeling of fear hammered at Kina's will and only the knowledge that death awaited the way she had come kept her feet moving.

Light was failing fast as the thick canopy high above blocked out the sun. The name 'Darkwood' was apt for such a place. This was not a place that welcomed strangers. It was beginning to resemble a cave deep within the earth.

Pausing, Kina strained to listen for her pursuers. They were closer now, no doubt gaining on her while she plodded along by her own feet. What she heard was not all bad, for she could hear no more galloping of horses. Those that chased her now did so by foot also, and did so at a pace that suggested great caution. They moved no quicker than a march and even as she listened they hesitated. Perhaps tales of these woods had reached Drago's ears as well.

Or perhaps it was the unnatural silence of this place unclaimed by man. It had been Drago that had taught her to be cautious when nature was scarce. Two scenarios were commonplace and she had witnessed each in her adventures. Either a predator was near, possibly one large enough to threaten a full grown man, or there was a darkling near. Creatures of the dark were fearsome and by far more dangerous than any natural predator. Kina had encountered wraiths before in tombs. They killed not for food, but instead seemingly for sport. No weapon of man could harm them. She had escaped the wraiths, but not to any amount of skill on her part.

The memory of wraiths instilled a new sense of wariness within Kina and she slowed to a stop to survey her surroundings more closely. Few rays of sunlight breached the high canopy to spill upon the dark ground and dried leaves. Still she heard nothing of wildlife, only the rustle of wind drifting between the trees. A glimmer of light caught her attention from amidst the tree trunks. It was gone by the time Kina focused on the area, but she held her ground and waited. There was danger in moving without thinking, and she wasn't going to risk herself needlessly.

The wait wasn't long before the wind kissed the leaves once more. While it must have been stronger above to make the noise it did, down where Kina stood it could be barely felt. It was, as it turned out, strong enough to illuminate danger. A long line of wispy material glistened in a ray of light as it vibrated in the air. Now that she spotted the thin line she traced it upward to the source. Gasping at what she saw, she stepped back away from the frightening sight. It was a spider web, like many she had seen in every town, cave and wood. The difference was this one was twenty paces high and perhaps twice as wide. The lines were secured tightly to the ground and through the canopy of the trees.

Knowing now what to look for Kina scanned her surroundings and noted that there were other swaths of spider silk strung high in the trees. They were behind her, above her, and all around. She didn't see any spiders, but she recognized that these were the predators of this forest. What they would eat, she didn't know, but the silence spoke of the respect the woodland creatures had for these arachnids.

She wondered if Drago had learned of this, or if he had shown such caution for yet another danger. She drew her small dagger from her belt and wielded it before her to ward off uncontrollable fears. If not for Drago, she would have time to investigate safe passage to negotiate the wood. The fact was now she would be hurried, and hastiness would cause her to make mistakes.

Swallowing deeply, Kina forced her feet to move once more. Wide-eyed and alert for danger, she pressed deeper into the wood. She kept her head low and tried to avoid the darker shadows where possible. She did not get very far before frightened yells behind her began. She could hear the cries of a youthful male, not one of Drago's men but perhaps a boy from the town seeking to prove his manhood. She hoped it was not the stable hand who had helped her. When his yell was calmed she heard the alarm go out to the others warning of the webs.

Kina looked at her surroundings once more. No doubt Drago would be doing much the same. His experiences would not permit him to be reckless in such a situation. Still no sign of the web-weavers. Calmed slightly, Kina considered the faint voices she was hearing. She could hear them clearly despite the distance that must have separated them. It seemed that her new ears were more sensitive than her old ones. Not a comforting thought, but for the moment useful.

A shriek made Kina jump, and she crouched lower to the ground. The boy was screaming now in panic, and accompanied by the yells and cries of others near him. "May Veran spare you from your fate," she whispered softly, finding no malice within her for the strangers. They acted out of misunderstanding and the danger she shared with them. It was Drago she found herself thinking most of. He should know that she was not a monster, yet he had instigated this chase.

Kina used their moment of confusion to distance herself from them further. She found another web soon enough. Her sleeve lightly snagged on an unseen thread which stuck fast. Wary of what dangers may lay in wait she dared not even breathe as she looked only with her eyes. A long silver line shimmering in a dying ray of light went up into the trees beyond her limited field of vision in her current position. It seemed to her there was only the one, but she did not allow herself to believe that she would safely pull free. The distant screams told her these were dangerous. Carefully, she raised her dagger before her eyes and slashed at the thread to clear her sleeve. As she had hoped, the blade swiped clear through. The sticky line snagged the hilt and tugged her arm into the air as the web snapped back like a released bow string. The dagger was ripped from her grasp and disappeared into the canopy. She tumbled heavily on the ground and quickly scrambled back to her feet.

Lesson learned, Kina thought to herself as she gasped for breath to refill her lungs. The webs were more dangerous than they appeared indeed. The lines were not to support the massive webs in the trees, but were stretched out to snag prey on the ground. Her knife was wrapped in numerous strands high above her head. Gone, she realized uneasily. That left her with the dead king's sword that Drago had wanted so badly. She'd never used a sword before. She doubted it would be any more use to her here than the dagger was.

There was movement in the shadows above her, forcing Kina to abandon thoughts of weapons. She picked her way carefully over the leaves, ever watchful for the sticky traps. She kept several paces between herself and any lines she encountered, watching each as if it would move. She picked up her pace, but remained cautious for any change in the environment.

Her wary eyes caught a glimmer of light so close that it made her flinch. She had nearly run headlong into another sticky strand. She took a step back and again looked around. It seemed hopeless to her. No wonder folk feared this place. How many had lost their lives here? Would she soon join the lost souls?

Hesitantly Kina took a step forward. It would do her little good to stay where she was. The only escape was to press forward and escape the woods before night fell. She needed to treat this danger as though it were one she discovered underground and be watchful.

Finding a large stick on the ground proved to be helpful as well. She waved it in front of her path wherever the shadows were too deep, looking for hidden spider lines. When that stick was snagged, she abandoned it and replaced it with a new one. After she had lost three, Kina began to gather any sticks she found and collected them under her arm so that she would not be caught without one. It was a slow but steady escape.

Drago's voice carried through the trees to her ears with just enough volume to still be heard. How long had she traveled? She must have covered half a league for him to have been so far.

"Kina!" he cried out again. "I'll hunt your tainted hide to the ends of the earth if I have to! I swear this! I will find you! Kina!"

Kina froze for a moment, fearing that he would spring out of the shadows to kill her. The facts as she saw them chased away that momentary fear. Drago was now far behind her and she would be free of the Darkwood long before he. Once under the sun again she would only increase her distance.

Chapter Three

As nightfall approached, Kina settled into the grassy fields beyond the Darkwood. She dared not stop until the woods were small and indistinct on the horizon. Alone, Kina wandered aimless in the fields. It took much of the remaining daylight for her to clear enough of the long grass and dig a small pit into the soft earth to even attempt lighting a fire. Even then, she found herself with only a pile of damp grass to burn and a few twisted roots. The resulting smoldering fire was not as warm as she had hoped for, nor as bright. It did create a fair bit of smoke that she hoped would at least keep the wildlife away.

The fire may not have been a success, but Kina didn't dwell on it. She had her first moments to relax since waking to Loor's angry face, and even if the firelight wasn't the best, she was determined to use this time to do something constructive. Failing to think of anything, she emptied her bag on the ground and took stock of her belongings again. She frowned at the objects she lay before her. She had a bit of money, though some of it had no value within this kingdom. She had a magic sword, an empty knife sheath, some rope and a bit of pitch to make torches with. Most of her clothing had been left in her remaining bags at the inn. Hungry, cold, and alone, Kina stared at her smoldering fire pit.

Her attention was suddenly drawn to the darkness. Something was coming, she could hear it in the grasses as it approached. She wished for the comforting presence of her dagger, even if she knew nothing of how to use it in a fight. The sounds were human, she realized as she picked out the tap of feet softly stepping over the ground. It was unlikely that this was one of her pursuers. Up to now, they had stayed together as a group and she doubted they would send out individuals alone at night to find her. She forced herself to relax and decided to confront her visitor on a different level.

"You may as well sit by the fire," she announced confidently. "It's not very good, but it's better than lurking about in the field at night."

The other hesitated, the movement disappearing and leaving only the whispering of a faint wind in the grass. It was long enough to cause doubt, Kina realized, but her hearing was getting better. She could hear the soft sigh of restrained breathing, and she looked toward the sound pointedly. The quiet didn't last and stealth was reluctantly abandoned. The grasses parted and a dark figure stepped into the light. His hair was a bit too long, but seemed well cared for, and there was a bit of scruff on his chin, suggesting to her that he had been well groomed before spending too much time away from town. He dressed in badly faded colors of Faneria, perhaps explaining why he had avoided taking the time out for a trim. The poor lighting made his skin look pale and dirty, but an odd lopsided grin on his face spoke of a healthy sense of humor.

"A young miss as well," he commented, shaking his head. "Fate must be smiling on me. I just might share your fire, and perhaps some dinner as well?"

"Sit," she offered generously, amused by his words and very relieved that he did not seem to notice her ears. He must have been only able to see her outline in the darkening night, and had so far not understood that she was not fully human. "But I'm afraid I have no food to share."

Kina noted the bow he carried, but his arrows were kept over his shoulder in his quiver still. She wondered if he was a Fanerian scout. She had heard many tales told of scouts and spies sent into the neighboring lands. She had little doubt that the warlords in Edan did the same.

"I see," he responded, nodding and dropping a good-sized bag from his shoulder. "Well, I may have enough. If you eat lightly." The man sighed and looked inside his bag. "It's a good thing Ishaw isn't more than a day from here."

Kina nodded, and decided to draw upon the stranger's knowledge of the land. "Which way is Ishaw from here?"

"Well," the man answered as he dug inside his sack, "it's south of here. Really, it's not that hard to find, but if you are heading that way you can join me." He retrieved some dried strips of meat and tossed her one. "Funny, I get the impression that you're experienced in the field, but you have no food and I've seen children start better fires. Of course, said children burned down the livery..." He shook his head and chuckled lightly at the joke or memory.

Kina bit off a chunk of the meat and chewed hard on the salted lump in her mouth. She'd never eaten anything like this before. She wasn't at all certain she liked it either, but she was hungry enough that she didn't care to decide.

"I see," the stranger said, as if her chewing was an answer. "Correct me if I'm wrong, but this is the first time you have traveled alone. Normally you travel with others."

Surprised by his insight, Kina nodded. She swallowed her bite and felt the lump as it sank all the way to her stomach. She winced at the way it settled, but forced a grateful smile to her face. "Thank you, this is good."

"Liar," he replied as he regarded his own stick. "Salted hopper meat."

Kina stopped herself from taking a second bite just before her teeth made contact with the meat and removed the strip from her mouth. "Are hoppers the small, slimy things that live in the swamps?"

"They live in many of the waterways. When prepared like this hopper meat will last forever." He laughed gently to himself. "And do you know why?"

She shook her head.

"Because nobody will eat it," he grumbled, moving as though he were about to throw his piece away. He hesitated before slowly slipping the uneaten portion back into his small bag. "I was really hoping you had food of your own. What have you got in that sack of yours?"

Regarding her bag, Kina considered the contents carefully. "Some clothes, a few trinkets. Nothing of any real value. I even lost my dagger in the Darkwood forest."

"You braved the Darkwood?" There was a pause. "On your own? Who are you?" There was honest interest now, and again Kina wondered if she should say the truth. This time she felt no harm could come of it.

"My name is Kina. Not long ago I traveled with Drago Kramoris."

He tensed sharply. "I've heard of him," the man said darkly. "An evil man, by all accounts. If you are a friend of his, then perhaps I should push on to Ishaw tonight."

"Wait," Kina started. "Don't leave me, please." Her visitor paused and regarded her through the firelight. Or tried to, she realized. She could see now that he was straining to see her through the dancing shadows created by the nearly dead fire. "Drago is a friend no longer," she stated simply. She was surprised how easily she could say it, despite the daggers she felt deep inside.

"I see," he said, though the friendly tone he had struck with her before was still absent.

She tried to find words to set her companion at ease. "I had to leave him recently. If he finds me, he will not hesitate to kill me. That was why I journeyed through the Darkwood."

The man paused a good few moments before settling down on the earth once more. "I suppose there is a story behind this. Perhaps you would like to tell it?"

"Not tonight," she answered uneasily.

"Fair enough." There was an odd sound in his voice when he spoke next. "Forgive me, but I'll ask again later. Not now, but I'm curious to learn why he would chase you."

Kina hesitated and thought quickly for a delaying tactic. "Then perhaps I should ask your name. A gentleman generally introduces himself before asking the name of the maiden."

"Maiden? Hah!" He laughed loudly. "But you're right, I have been rude. Daven Hitchcliffe," he answered, leaning over deeply in as much of a mock bow as he could manage while sitting. "At your service, fair lady."

Kina stifled a laugh at his performance. "Should I have heard of you?"

He shrugged. "Perhaps of my family. Perhaps not. I could believe those of Edan would not have heard of the Hitchcliffes of Faneria. A companion of Drago Kramoris perhaps would be traveled enough to know it. That band of tomb raiders has a black trail that leads back and forth across these lands."

"Sorry," Kina answered.

Daven shrugged. "Alas, my family is better known in Faneria."

"I grew up in Faneria," Kina replied, a bitterness creeping into her voice.

"Ouch," Daven remarked, dramatically placing his hand over his heart. "My homeland slighted by the young miss. I take it you've no love for your place of birth?"

"I suppose it's not that bad," she responded. The moment of darkness she had felt for her homeland disappeared as she smiled at Daven's antics. She was grateful for the company. She wondered how he would react in the morning when the sun revealed the monster she really was. She took pleasure in the moment she had.

"Is your family really famous?" she asked.

Daven shrugged. "The name is known within certain circles, I would imagine. Generations of loyal service to the kingdom has brought some recognition within the courts of noble lords."

"If you're a royal scout, you take great risk traveling these lands," Kina commented. "You must be very brave."

The comment must have caught him off guard, as he suddenly appeared uncomfortable. "Uh, well. Of course." He sighed and looked at the dying fire with a haunted look.

Pausing only a moment, Kina refused to let the awkward silence remain. "Well, being alone so far from home, wearing the colors of Faneria, I consider you brave."

Daven stared at her through the shadows, not quite being able to focus on her. Reluctantly, he shifted his feet and lay down on the ground using his sack to cushion his head. "I suggest you get some sleep. Ishaw can be a little rough."

Dismissal, Kina realized. It was spoken as being helpful, but she understood the meaning. Daven had grown tired of talking to her on this topic and had chosen to shut her out completely. It served as a reminder to her that she was alone. She needed to find somebody soon who could change her back.

Kina lay herself on the ground and whispered a silent prayer to Veran. Then she too tried to get some rest.

Kina was awakened by the sounds of movement near to her. It was still dark, but the gentle glow on the horizon spoke of a bright day coming. Used to such invasions of her privacy, she easily focused on her intruder without alerting him of her wakefulness. It took a moment to register that this was not one of Drago's men, but instead a stranger. The cool night air was still and Kina thought pensively about who this one could be.

The stranger pulled an old aged sword from her bag and she remembered all from the day previous. She could remain silent no longer.

"I would be careful with that."

Daven started and backed away from her quickly, taking the sword with him. "You're awake." It wasn't so much a question as much as perhaps an unhappy realization that he had been caught.

"I am."

"Well, it would be good to get an early start on the day." Daven answered, no hint of uneasiness in his voice. She wondered how he could be so bold as to lie to her face while holding one of her belongings in front of him. "I was just looking for some food."

"That sword is not for cutting dried hopper meat," Kina remarked dryly.

He froze in the darkness for just a moment. He looked down at the sword and tilted it, as if testing to see how it reflected the light of the stars. He smiled back at her after he was satisfied with his test. "You are good," he commented. "How much can you see in the dark?"

"Enough," she answered tightly. "For your own sake, please put that sword down. If you are looking for something to steal, I have perhaps a few coins, but at this moment that sword is of greater danger to you than I."

"What, this?" he asked, undaunted by her warnings. He twisted his hands and tossed the blade into the air and with a deft move caught it in his palm once more. It was an impressive display, but Kina did not take pleasure in it. Daven's confident smile shone but for a moment, before he yelped and released his grip. The sword hit the dirt and lay still, but Kina noted the faint aura of deep colored light that encircled it.

"What in Fate's Name is that?" Daven questioned as he backpedaled.

"A weapon that predates the walls of Brighton." She calmly stood and approached the blade.

"I heard a voice," Daven told her. "In my mind. I did not recognize the tongue, but it did not speak in pleasant tones." He regarded her through the pre-dawn shadows and backed away. His eyes grew larger, perhaps seeing her for what she was at long last. "What are you?"

She bent over and collected the sword, but the blade didn't speak for her as it had for Daven. Instead it was as dead as the king it was stolen from. "I'm what this sword wished me to be," she answered. Daven was still backing away and she sought for a way to placate him. She decided upon the truth that he had sought during the night.

"You wished to know why Drago would kill me, perhaps now you know. Two days ago I was as human as you are. The intention was to sell this sword to the Duke of Deverell. Then, while holding the sword, a strange magic transformed me into this…" She wondered how to describe herself other than 'monster.' "Drago gathered the townsfolk and chased me out of Brighton into the Darkwood."

Daven hesitated to speak and fell silent, no doubt wondering the details she had neglected. It was becoming lighter now and he could see her clear enough to see that she was mostly human. When he finally spoke, his question seemed strange to Kina. "Is there any particular reason you wish to travel to Ishaw?"

She blinked in response before finding words for her answer. "I didn't know where Ishaw was before you told me. I was simply running, nothing more."

Daven nodded and considered her words. "Like much of Edan, Ishaw is deeply religious. Items of magic frighten them and they do not like strangeness. For your sake, if what you say is true, you best not be seen in Ishaw."

She nodded sadly. "But I have nowhere to go."

Daven looked uncomfortable at her plea. He looked away, though she knew that he was thinking more about the future than about the terrain. "You don't want to come with me," he told her at long last. "While I may not be as notorious as your last companions, I am no Fanerian scout."

"Given what I have told you, do you think I am concerned about you stealing my possessions? I have none worth taking but the sword, and that frightens you near as much as it scares me."

"I want nothing to do with magic," he stated firmly. "My life is too complicated for the troubles magic is storied to bring."

"Would you allow me to travel with you if I volunteer my services to you?"

Daven looked surprised by her offer. He chuckled darkly before flashing a grin at her that was thick with hidden meaning. "What could you possibly offer me?"

"The same services that Drago Kramoris found indispensable. I'm a treasure hunter. I may even know more about the dangers involved than you yourself, and you are a veteran adventurer."

"I doubt that," he answered, but he looked over his shoulder the same. "You did travel through the Darkwood, however… Listen, Kina, to stay with me is to place further risk on your life."

"My life is worth little until I can lift this curse. I accept the risk if you will accept me."

Daven considered her words carefully. He stood still, looking once more to the south. Then, silently he gathered his bag, quiver and bow and began to walk in the direction of Ishaw. Kina didn't hesitate; she grabbed her bag and stuffed the sword in while she hurried after him.

"You're going to need a mage," Daven told her as she fell into step beside him. "One that will help you. Given the rarity of those who know anything worthwhile about magic, you could have a long search ahead of you. I can take you as far as Ishaw, but I make no promise to help you further."

Kina nodded silently, accepting his comments as fact.

"I need to do something about those ears of yours," Daven noted with an unhappy sigh. "And that tail. You are liable to get us both killed. Have you a cloak?"

"No. Nothing like that," she answered unhappily.

Daven shot her an odd look. "What do you wear during the winter? Or the rains?"

"Whatever I'm given," she replied sharply. "I didn't plan on being changed."

"Sorry," Daven mumbled back. It was odd for her to hear those words spoken to her as such. "I have a cloak, nothing fancy mind you, but it will do. Next we stop I'll give it to you to use."

"Thank you."

"You are welcome," Daven stated before looking skyward. "How do I get myself into these messes?"

Kina chose not to answer. She smiled to herself at the small change in her luck.

Ishaw, as it turned out, was not a city. It was a town at best, really no more than a small settlement. She noted there were fewer buildings than Brighton and none of the grand buildings popular among the nobles. People here were simple farmers and those required to support them. And the entire village, it seemed, took interest in her as she walked down the quiet streets alongside Daven.

"I feel silly," she told Daven quietly. The cloak was large and dark, and with the hood pulled over her head on a bright and sunny day she had little doubt that she had crossed the realms of unusual into peculiar. Admittedly, she doubted anybody had noticed either ears or tail. The sword she now wore at her side only added to her discomfort. She was unused to wearing a weapon, and the sword seemed longer to her now that it hung from her belt. It seemed to brush against her knee in a way that she worried might become a tripping hazard.

"You look fine," he answered, looking about warily. She knew the signs, he was nervous as well.

"I look strange."

Daven sighed and shook his head. "Actually, you look like a warrior from the lands of Zahn far to the east."

"A warrior?" Kina repeated uncertainly as she stared furiously at Daven from beneath the hood.

"Assassin is more the word, I suppose." He shrugged.

"I do not look like an assassin!" Kina hissed.

"We're not dead yet, are we?" Daven grinned back at her with a look she was fast associating with him. It gave him a sort of uncertainty and nervousness that she found refreshing. "Besides, I doubt any of these simple folk would see the similarities."

Kina noted the way Daven tensed and likewise took caution. A big man had just stepped away from one of the buildings and stood in their way expectantly. He was a powerful looking man, broader in the shoulders than even Drago. He wore leather armor, though laced with small metal plates that seemed to be sewn into it. His stern gaze focused solely on Daven, allowing Kina to silently distance herself from Daven to provide any space he may need to move quickly.

"I have had to track across most of Edan to find you, Daven," the big man stated angrily as he stomped forward. Daven gave ground and raised his hands to placate the large man.

"Now, now, let's not be rash Lyle," Daven remarked nervously.

"Too late for that. There is a price on your head now."

Daven looked shocked. "Who?"

The big man scowled and drew his sword. It was a large, broad blade, but the big man carried it in a single hand as though it weighed nothing. Either it was well crafted, Kina guessed, or Lyle was a very strong man. Either way, she prepared herself to jump to Daven's aid. She just wasn't sure how she was to do that.

"You stole from the Earl of Marrows."

"Oh," Daven answered, looking uncertain. "It was only a few gold pieces. He's overreacting a bit, don't you think so?"

"And then you burnt down half the castle in your escape."

"I forgot about that," Daven replied. His answer angered the larger man more.

"Are you going to come with me, or not?" he asked as he continued to close the ground between them. Unskilled or not, Kina had maneuvered herself into position to help Daven. If anything, she could certainly serve as a distraction. She drew her sword as Lyle was about to walk past her. Or she was going to, had it not been for the tip of his sword pointing at her by the time she had hers half way drawn.

"Kina! Stop!" Daven's voice stilled her hand, but she remained focused on the large man. She noted now that he had similar features to Daven, despite the differences in size. They both had the same sharp jaw lines, and the prominent nose. The beard had softened the features on this one, but she could see the contours now that she was up close.

"Well," Lyle said slowly as he carefully measured his words, "are you going to introduce me to your assassin?"

Kina felt the warmth of anger flush through her at being called an assassin, but she did not allow herself to completely back down. She did, however, put her sword back and removed her hand from it very slowly. She hoped she wasn't trembling.

"Sorry, Lyle, were you saying something?" Daven's mocking question, mixed with the hushed whispers of the watching crowd, combined to give the moment for Kina a surreal quality. Lyle kept his eyes on her warily but lowered his weapon. She breathed a sigh of relief.

"I see your choice in friends has not changed," Lyle stated to Daven, despite his focus on her.

"You, of course, know what is best," Daven returned unhappily.

"Who is she?"

Before Daven could answer, Kina spoke up. "My name is Kina Ukiel, and I am not an assassin."

"Of course," Lyle answered in a tone that suggested he had little faith in her words. "Most women of this land carry swords and find need to hide beneath their cloaks during the light of day."

This time Daven interrupted her. "Lyle, this is not the place or time for introductions. Somebody has probably alerted the town guard."

Kina looked about, realizing the truth in Daven's words and feeling a fresh fear for her safety.

Lyle likewise saw reason and after a moment spent glaring at Daven, put his own sword away. Once more Kina was taken by his size. He was two heads taller than she and being so close forced her to look up to see his face.

"Come on Lyle," Daven said as he brushed past the big man without concern. Kina hesitated as Lyle glared at her once more, then he turned to follow Daven. She followed him, mindful to keep out of reach should things threaten to become violent once more. Daven led them to the first tavern in sight and quickly slipped in without another look at his surroundings. Lyle ducked his head when he entered the door and Kina hesitantly stepped into building after them.

There was a greater feeling of privacy inside than there was in the streets. With only a handful of patrons, the place was for the most part quiet and secluded. It was strangely comforting compared to the last tavern she had been in. She supposed that the place was busier at other times of the day, but her curiosity was a small distraction that was dismissed easily. Daven and Lyle sat on opposite ends of a table. Silently she took to Daven's left and sat down lightly.

"Did the puppet master order you out here, or did you cut the strings?" Daven's question was laced with venom, though not directed to Lyle.

"What did our family do to deserve a curse like you?" Lyle's anger seemed to deflate into frustration and the big man buried his face in his hands. It was a strange sight to behold.

"The Hitchcliffe line had too much pride," Daven answered with a triumphant smile. "I take it the captain is still upset about..."

"Yes, yes. Father took it personally when you disappeared." There was a hint of scolding and a touch of anger in the elder brother's voice.

"I looked bad in armor."

"You will look worse with a rope around your neck," Lyle argued and Daven suddenly lost interest in the entire topic. He looked at Kina and she wondered what it was in his eyes that made him appear sad. Clearly there was some history between the two, and she was guessing there was blood shared, but they were dropping enough information to draw her curiosity without providing any answers.

"Why did you come?" Daven asked Lyle as he looked to the big man once more. This time there were no undertones in his voice suggesting humor or barbs.

"The captain ordered your return, dead if necessary."

"I see," Daven answered darkly.

"It is not like that," Lyle hissed. "You left him no choice. You left a path of destruction that surpassed that of the last great war. And you can bet he was under a lot of watchful eyes to see how he would react to the actions of his own son."

"He had a choice and he made it. Why are you here, Lyle? Did he send you to test your loyalty?"

"I volunteered," Lyle snapped back. "I wanted to bring you back alive before anybody put a sword in your gut."

"Nice to see you care," Daven replied. "There doesn't seem to be much for me in Faneria these days."

"Of course," Lyle sneered. "You can soil our name here with your woman without ever facing the consequences of your actions."

Kina contained her anger, but she found she didn't shrink away as she did when she was insulted in Drago's company. Daven's response let it be clear that he was not going to let the insult slip either.

"You let your temper guide you, Lyle," Daven hissed. "There's more here than you can see. There's magic at work here. Even you must see that." He paused, though not long enough to give Lyle time to speak. "What do you know of Parn Gawthrain?"

Kina's ears perked up beneath her hooded cloak, and she noted the change in Lyle's expression, though she didn't know what it meant.

"The Mad Duke of Deverell," Lyle whispered back warily. His eyes rested upon her suspiciously. "I know enough to be cautious in his domain," the big man said finally.

"Is the Captain aware that he's chasing down magic talismans?"

"No," Lyle answered firmly. "And no good could come of such searches. Are you certain of this?"

Kina gave Daven no room to answer for her. "Very certain," she said firmly. "I have personally seen the Duke attempt to purchase a magic sword."

Lyle's regard for her had not improved, but he did seem to reevaluate her. "And who are you?"

"Kina Ukiel, of Windermere." She took the name of her home town back into her identity with hopes it would help to placate the elder brother.

"So this time you say Windermere. I still do not know you. Why do you wear the hood indoors, Kina Ukiel? Are you part of some mage sect that demands it?"

"Personal safety," she answered, finding some humor in her own response. "When Ishaw is behind me, I shall remove the cloak."

"Fair enough," Lyle answered, giving Daven a questionable look. "But how can you tell that the sword that Gawthrain was trying to purchase was magical?"

"The magic is the reason I wear this cloak," she answered, trying to be truthful without coming out and saying she was now a monster. If Daven regarded this man with some measure of respect, she would show him the same. "I have the sword still, though I need to find a mage who can unlock its secrets."

Lyle and Daven both remained silent at that. She waited patiently as they seemed to communicate with each other through looks and scowls.

At last Daven spoke again, and did so with a calmer voice. "I have not agreed to help," he said for all to hear, "but I do find interest in anything that the Duke of Deverell decides important enough to deal for in person. As should Faneria."

Lyle nodded unhappily. "If the Duke wants for the sword, then he should not get his hands on it."

Kina smiled brightly at their words. It hadn't occurred to her that she had hoped so much for their acceptance, but she felt buoyed by their support. "So you will help me?"

"Certainly," Daven answered, flashing a grin at her. "We could never leave a damsel in such distress."

"That is the most absurd thing I have ever heard said," Lyle retorted, looking at his brother pointedly.

"Well, okay. You probably would abandon her."

Lyle sighed and looked at Kina. He seemed to be trying to see more of her beneath the shadows of the hood, but relented with a simple nod. "Where your needs fall in line with my own duties, I shall follow. You wish to find out what this sword does, and I find that I, too, am curious why the Duke wants for magic. When we have discovered what this sword is, and know what dangers it presents, I will return to Faneria with Daven."

"Wonderful!" Daven proclaimed loudly, seeming to Kina that he had missed the final point his brother had made. "We need to find a magic user," Daven continued without slowing down.

"It is not like ancient days when magic was commonplace," the bigger man said thoughtfully before seeking out Daven's eyes with his own. "You are more familiar with this land, Daven," Lyle acknowledged reluctantly.

"True, but I haven't come across any magic users. Kina?"

"None," she answered truthfully.

"We could return to Faneria. Perhaps somebody at the royal temples could be of help."

Daven spoke first in disapproval before Kina's mouth opened to give her assent. "Dangerous. The Agaesi are likely to treat Kina as a monster."

"Monster?" Lyle repeated, his eyes moving back to Kina's cloak.

"Who are the Agaesi?" Kina asked. She had heard some odd tales of armored knights traveling within the realm of Faneria, but it wasn't something that had interested her.

"An elite guard, usually tasked with missions of great importance," Lyle told her, though he was already giving his brother a scolding look as though expecting Daven's follow up.

"They deal with things that cannot be explained within nature. Magic and monsters."

"That is only rumor," Lyle snorted. "I fail to see why they would be interested in her."

"Kina should decide," Daven argued, ignoring his brother. "It's her life that's on the line here."

Kina frowned as she found the two different men turn to her and await her decision. It was clear that they both wanted for different answers and that she could not please both. In fact, she wasn't at all certain she could please either of them.

"Maybe it's best if you make the decisions," she responded hesitantly.

"Kina," Daven said slowly, "You know more about this sword than either of us. Tell us what you feel is the right path."

Taking a deep breath, Kina struggled with her decision. If it were just herself, she would have decided to remain in Edan, perhaps even returning to Brighton. She sought for a reason why she hesitated in saying so still and found only her fears of disappointing her new companions. She looked at Daven first and then his brother before nodding her assent to the situation. "I think we should stay in Edan. The closer to Brighton, the better."

"Brighton," Lyle muttered unhappily.

"That seems rather risky," Daven agreed.

"Unless either of you have heard of a people with long ears?" She waited while the pair exchanged confused looks. Hearing nothing, she continued with strength. "The owner of this sword was buried in a temple beneath Brighton. The great walls were made from blocks removed from the old temple, destroying all trace above ground, but this was a temple filled with markings and statues showing a people not seen in these parts for many lifetimes. Now, I've heard stories of such people before in regions to the south of here near the border of Faneria. Long-eared strangers who disappeared on ships that traveled beyond the horizon." The brothers looked at her as if she had grown another appendage. She assumed it was more likely her story that caused their reaction and not another magical addition to her body, though she did feel her tail twitch beneath the fabric of the cloak. "These are legends. I don't know how much truth is in them."

The pair seemed to digest her words carefully. They seemed

suitably chastised for doubting her reasons, but no less troubled. Daven found his voice first. "Long ears, such as yours?"

"Unfortunately, not. At least I could've passed for human then," she grumbled. "And they didn't have tails either."

"Lyle?"

Lyle started at Daven's prompting. Kina noted that he seemed to have been studying her after her last admission. He shifted uneasily before leaning back into his chair. "You are talking of a people gone since the Time of Gods and Magic. I have heard nothing from those times but stories made for the ears of children. Real knowledge of such times could be harder to come by than a magic user." Lyle paused again and considered the scenario carefully. "You are going to need somebody who knows the land, in addition to a magic user to interpret the sword." Lyle marked each point on his fingers.

"And to cure me," Kina added firmly.

Lyle looked at her questioningly but let her comment slide so that he could continue his list. "You are going to need money to support such an expedition. And you have got to do all this while in hiding from the power within the realm." He was at four points and was making a show that these were starting to add up against her.

"And a band of rogue mercenaries," Daven added helpfully. Lyle glared across the table at his brother, but lifted his thumb to indicate the additional requirement.

"You would do better taking the sword to Faneria and hiding from the likes of the Duke."

"Lyle, it's not that simple," remarked Daven.

"I can't live like this," Kina pleaded. "My appearance frightens people."

Lyle reacted immediately, moving forward and pulling her hood down before she could react. In the moment that followed it seemed to Kina that time had stopped. Lyle remained still, the hood still within his hand as he stared at her. She noted that Daven was holding onto Lyle's arm, not quite able to prevent the hood from being removed. Lyle showed little emotion. There was a brief widening of the eyes, and then he was looking about at the other patrons. Daven scrambled to put the hood back into place while Kina tried to calm her racing heart.

"Nobody saw?" Daven asked his brother as he too joined in the uncertain search of the bar.

"I would not put my life to that," Lyle answered darkly. "We best put some distance between ourselves and this town." He rose quickly, surprising Kina by his abruptness.

Daven tugged on her cloak to get her attention. "We need to leave," he told her. She was pleased that he did not seem angry.

"Sorry," she whispered as she took his hand and stood.

"The damage is done, and there will be a time for regrets later," Daven told her. "Besides, you're not at fault for this. For now, we should be moving. We still have a bit to do before we put Ishaw behind us."

Kina nodded. "I understand."

Lyle waited for them outside, looking uneasy, but she got the impression that he was not frightened by what he had seen. Daven had reacted with greater emotion than had Lyle, and he now seemed at ease with her presence.

"We need horses," Daven said to his brother. "And supplies."

"I have some, but you would do well to find yourself a horse. To the east you will find a single white tree shading the only water hole to be seen for leagues."

"I know of it," Daven confirmed. "About half a day's walk from here."

"I will meet you there. Be warned, I will drag your beaten hide back to Faneria if you do not show by sundown." Lyle turned and walked away, but Daven seemed unconcerned by his brother's quick departure. He seemed more concerned with her.

                    J. R. Dwornik

"The cloak may no longer be enough to disguise you here," he commented as he appraised her appearance. "Can you use that sword?"

"What?"

"Can you use it if your life was threatened? You looked afraid when you tried to draw your sword on Lyle."

Kina felt disheartened by Daven's observations. She had hoped that she appeared fairly threatening when she thought Lyle was a danger to them.

"Forgive me if I fail to frighten, but I was never a soldier."

"You were a mercenary. Is there any weapon you've used?"

Uncomfortable now, Kina looked about unhappily. She thought about her encounter with Loor. "I have used the sword to defend myself on one occasion. I try to avoid confrontation when possible."

Daven shook his head in disapproval. "We'll have to do something about that."

"What?" Kina's alarm drove pleading into her voice. "What does that mean?"

"Later," Daven told her distractedly. He seemed to be watching a group of six soldiers arriving on horseback. They moved at a slow trot, looking both graceful and intimidating at the same time. They didn't seem overly concerned about finding anybody, which did little to relax Kina's nerves. Daven chuckled darkly and turned to her again with a strange grin on his face. "Hold these," he said, thrusting his bow and quiver at her. He bent down and grabbed some of the fine dirt from the road in his hands. "Keep your head down, and be ready."

As the soldiers filed into another tavern, Daven made his way across the street. One soldier remained outside, apparently guarding their rides. The soldier in polished armor stood with a long pike and watched those that strayed too near with an untrusting eye. Daven's approach was of course noticed, but gained little more attention than any other of the townsfolk.

Despite the watchful eye, Daven passed by the guard at just barely arms reach. At the last moment he moved quickly, turning with a fist full of sand thrown into the face of the soldier. The guard yelped and swung the pike blindly at Daven, but he moved faster, twisting beneath the swing and then grabbing onto the weapon close to the soldier's hands. A quick twist and it was Daven who was armed. Rather than swinging the blade, Daven drove the blunt end of the weapon forward into the guard's face. The violence in the action wasn't as obvious as the sound that Kina heard from the impact.

Before the soldier had even hit the ground Daven was already freeing one of the horses with the blade. Kina watched wide-eyed as the rest of the soldiers started to come out the door, swords drawn. Daven flung the pike at the door and rushed along beside the horse. The pike caused the soldiers to hesitate, and that was all Daven had apparently needed to get onto the horse.

Kina stood blinking in shock as he raced towards her on the back of the stolen horse. "Kina!" She started, realizing Daven had yelled to her, and he leaned towards her with one arm out to grab her. She swung the quiver over her shoulder and readied herself. Daven slowed the horse to a stop. The horse seemed huge to her, larger than the one she had stolen from Brighton. Daven pulled her up in front of him before immediately kicking the horse into a fast run again.

His hand found hers still tightly gripped around his bow. "I need the bow," he shouted in her ear. "Take the reins."

She fumbled at the leather straps he forced into her hands. She grabbed them and huddled over the horse, afraid she would fall off. Unlike the last one, this one seemed wild and violent. Her hood caught the wind and flew back, leaving her hair to blow in the wind. The townsfolk parted ahead of her and watched wide-eyed as they passed.

She felt something slide off her back and looked over her shoulder to see Daven draw an arrow in his bow while facing back the way they had come. She saw the soldiers on their own horses galloping angrily after them. Daven's bow creaked loudly as it flexed, but he released the arrow so quickly Kina didn't have much chance to see. She was too busy trying to coax the horse through the last of the streets and out of Ishaw.

"Head south!" Daven's order came as he pulled another arrow from the quiver on her back.

She wanted to question his actions, but she was too frightened to do so. Instead, she simply followed his commands and pulled on the reins to relay his commands to the horse. It swung its head unhappily but did as she asked.

Behind her the bow flexed again, and this time she caught sight of the arrow in flight as she chanced a look. She was stunned to see that Daven found his mark despite being bounced about on the back of a horse. One of the soldiers caught the arrow in the shoulder and tipped backwards off his horse. Only three riders remained, and they were further slowed as Daven's next arrow whistled past them. Kina hadn't even been aware he had drawn another one.

"Hold us steady on this path for a bit," Daven ordered. "We'll head east once we've lost them. If they are going to find us, I want them to work for it."

They rode hard for several minutes longer, but it wasn't long before the town and the remaining soldiers were beyond sight. Between the hills and Daven's arrows, they were able to escape with relative ease. All the while Kina drew alarming parallels between Daven and Drago. A thief she had no qualms with, but the violence she had witnessed spoke of great skill and little restraint. She pulled the cloak's hood back up over her head and kept close to the horse as they continued away from Ishaw.

Chapter Four

It was late when they finally caught up on Lyle. True enough, he sat beneath the only tree amidst the grassy hills and large stones. His big horse, tied to a low branch, chewed on the grass but appeared to be loaded and ready for a quick ride if necessary. The full canopy offered a shady spot to settle and it appeared that Lyle had spent at least one night previous there. A small, burned out fire pit marked the ground like a blemish with blackened wood and ash in its center.

Lyle stood as they approached, and the dark scowl on his face showed that he was unhappy about something. Kina said as much to Daven, curious as to why his brother would look angry.

"It is his nature," Daven remarked in a flat tone. "Lyle believes in following the rules, even when they are wrong and unjust."

"And you not so much," Kina observed, thinking of their escape.

Daven sniffed in an amused manner. "Not so much."

"For brothers, you're two very different men."

"My mother was but a mistress the captain took after his wife died. It was a brief affair, but lasted long enough to gift the captain with another son, though it would seem my blood is not as pure as my brother." There were some darker underlying tones to Daven's voice. Kina didn't press further on the topic.

                    J. R. Dwornik

"I do not imagine," Lyle began gruffly as they got closer, "that this horse cost you as much as it should have."

"It'll cost me plenty if I have to hear you complain about it," Daven responded before looking over at Kina with a sly grin.

Being used as a distraction made her uncomfortable. She slid off the horse and landed solidly on the ground. Almost immediately the two returned to their verbal battle. Kina appreciated that the two brothers had their differences, but once again she seemed forgotten and cast aside by those she traveled with. She tossed off the cloak and stretched out. It felt good to be free of the heavy garment. She was beginning to realize that hiding a tail for prolonged periods was an uncomfortable practice. Kina leaned her back against the old tree as she gazed into the distance. It was peaceful, she thought as she purposefully ignored the brothers arguing. She found herself smiling despite her situation as her thoughts drifted back to the poor servant girl. This was what she was missing as she hid within the walls of Brighton. In many places the grasses here would reach Kina's knees, but there were numerous trails and openings that were worn down by travel. The water hole Lyle had noted back at the inn was a mere pond that appeared to be shallow and muddy, but from the sounds there were a few hoppers that called it home. Other areas were open where rocky outcroppings stuck out from the ground.

Her gaze lingered on one such outcropping and her smile faded. The rocks seemed fairly regular in shape, though worn down by ages of rain and wind. She pushed off from the tree and took a pair of strides toward them. How was it that a civilization had lived here long enough that they could build stone temples, and yet be forgotten to those who now lived in this land? Could they have called this water hole home as well?

"Daven?" She didn't look to see if he had heeded her voice. "Was there ever a settlement here?"

Daven seemed confused by her question. "Ishaw?"

"No," Kina said firmly. "Lyle?"

"None that I have heard spoken of."

Kina looked over her shoulder at the two brothers, both looking to be curious but lost by her question. She smiled at them and wondered what their reaction would be if she were right. "If you want to continue catching up, be my guest, but I am going to explore those rocks over there."

Lyle shrugged while Daven looked uncertain. "What's so special about those rocks?"

"That's what I want to know," she answered firmly. She knew what she wanted to find, another forgotten chamber containing the secrets to the sword she carried with her. It was unlikely at best, but she would never find an answer to her curse without looking. "Fair enough," she told them as she saw their hesitation. "I'll go alone while you two beat some sense into each other."

She only had a few steps on them before Daven called out for her to wait. She turned and put a hand on her hip impatiently. "Yes?"

"I'll come. Anything is better than bickering with this mule."

Lyle crossed his arms and glared down upon Daven's back as the younger brother picked his way over the uneven ground. Not wanting to anger him further, Kina relayed her invite to Lyle more personally.

"Lyle, you would be welcome to come along as well."

He merely looked away, looking as though he thought her as little more than some flighty village girl. Kina hoped that the animosity between the two wouldn't cause serious trouble in the future.

"Come along," Daven said softly as he came close. She wasn't sure she wanted to know what darkness tainted his words. "The puppet needs a moment to untangle his strings."

Kina hesitated a moment before nodding in acceptance. Perhaps Lyle did need a moment to himself to calm down. That wasn't the first time Daven had referred to Lyle as a puppet, however, and Kina was beginning to wonder what more was there between the two. Would she have developed as complex a relationship with her own brother had she remained on that farm so long ago?

Then she realized that any relationship she had would be complicated until she removed this curse.

"That was pretty sharp," Daven commented, bringing her away from the darkness within her own mind. "You're pretty bold to interrupt an argument like that."

"Not really," she answered. "Being able to argue like that takes plenty more than I have to give. I only offered a distraction."

Daven snorted indignantly. "Now you're just being modest. You've shown plenty of spirit since I crossed paths with you. Hells, you confronted me directly while I was trying to rob you blind in the middle of the wilderness. There are few women in this world who would do more than scream for help."

"Not that screaming would help," Kina remarked darkly. "We were alone in a field leagues away from anybody."

"Had I been the murderous type, you would have been in trouble."

"Had you been the murderous type, I would have been in familiar company. Do not misunderstand me. I still don't know you, however, I give you my trust that you will not intentionally bring me harm."

"And what would you like to know of me?"

Kina knew the playful tone in his voice was supposed to amuse her, but she only found it more concerning. "Daven, I've witnessed you steal and kill. Your arguments with your brother aside, you do all this with indifference. At least with Drago I knew when he was in a killing mood."

Daven reeled as if struck. Honest emotions were quickly quashed beneath his anger as he stopped walking to face her.

"Don't ever compare me to that monster again. Do you hear me? You know nothing about me!"

She flinched, but drew strength to put a few short words together. "That was my point."

He sighed heavily and looked skyward. "Do you really see me as a killer?"

"I met you only a day ago, and that incident in Ishaw paints a bleak picture."

With a huff, Daven shrugged and looked across the dry grassy hills. "Kina, you would do well remembering who those soldiers answer to. You would have less sympathy if you had seen what I've seen men wearing that armor do to folk they are to protect. People in all uniforms, not just those of Edan."

"I have seen plenty of evil, my soul will not be further burdened by your stories."

Daven looked to her and gave her a reluctant nod. "I suppose you have." Whatever shadows he was trying to hide drifted through his eyes briefly before he once more buried them within. "For me to tell them without you knowing me would provide some interesting contradictions. Come, we have rocks to claim."

She allowed for the simple tactic to work, and agreed. "Hopefully something more," she added.

"More than rocks?"

"Much more," she answered with a smile. "Rocks have secrets and stories too."

"I can't imagine it's much of a story. 'Today I sat here in the sun. Yesterday it rained.'"

"You laugh," Kina answered with a thin smile, "but often that is the story they tell. Only rocks tell stories in spans of centuries, not days. Most stones are boring, much like people, but there are a few that speak of forgotten times."

"Am I one of the boring people?" There was that playful tone again, trying to amuse her.

"That would not be a word I would use to describe you, no." She grinned at the very thought. "Most folk I have met are too afraid to venture far from their homes and will spend much of their lives within a few days from the place of their birth."

"You will find that they too can have their stories. Plenty more interesting than a bunch of old rocks."

"Perhaps," Kina answered doubtfully. By now, she could see that the rocks were indeed more than a random pile left by nature. The rocks were uniformly placed, though badly aged and long since collapsed. She smiled to herself over her unexpected find.

"Okay," Daven said as he noted the peculiar pile as if for the first time, "something is really strange here."

"It's a building," Kina told him as she picked up the pace. She jogged ahead of Daven and began to poke her head around in hopes of finding something more substantial. There was no writing apparent, and no clear indication of where the entrance would have been. "Help me to find a way inside."

"Inside?" Daven cursed loudly. "Kina, it's a pile of rocks. There is no inside anymore."

Kina paused and glared at Daven from atop an awkward pile. "Look, when walls made with stone blocks of this size collapse, they do not tend to fill in the spaces between. Furthermore, many of the ruins I have explored were partially buried beneath the surface. What you see tends to be little more than a small sample of what may lay beneath."

Daven cursed again, this time invoking the name of Fate. Feeling a bit playful now that she had a ruin to explore, she grinned at the thief with a teasing smile. "Careful of the names you call here. This may have been a temple to one of the gods." She leaned her head into a gap between stones and peered into the darkness within. It was definitely more open inside than it would appear. "Can you get me a torch?"

"Where am I going to find a torch?"

"Never mind. I have some pitch. I'll make one back at camp later."

Kina's eyes began to adjust to the light and she spotted a small, collapsed cavern within. There wasn't much room, but she could pass the obstructions easily enough. She just needed to find enough of a gap to get beyond the rocks. She climbed over the structure, pausing at any gap larger than her hand to peer inside. All the while she realized that Daven merely watched and grumbled as she worked. She decided to involve him a bit more. At least he might be able to help.

"If you could give me a hand, I am just looking for a gap big enough to slide in." She reached in an arm and swung it around inside without making contact with anything. "There is enough room inside and I can see a tunnel."

"You're a strange one," Daven remarked and reluctantly began to pick his way around the ruins. "What would you like me to do?"

She paused and considered what the next best option was. "The tunnel leads that way," she said, pointing in the vague direction that the hole seemed to lead. "See if there are any natural cave-ins that may have opened."

"You want me to look for a big hole in the ground."

"Well, a little one." Kina frowned in concentration and she levered herself around a stone into position to slide inside. It was definitely a tight fit. She wondered for a moment if she would get stuck, but began to push herself inside anyway. "Hold on, I might be able to get in here."

"Hey!" Daven's yell gave her little pause. "You be careful over there."

"This is nothing," she remarked with pride. She wiggled her shoulders and pulled herself through up to her chest. It was definitely a squeeze, but there was just enough room to shift her way through. She paused as she heard a sound much like a drumbeat echo up to her ears. The sound didn't repeat itself.

"What was that?" she asked, hoping her voice would be heard clearly.

"The ground," came Daven's muffled response. "It sounds hollow here." The beat echoed again, three times more. Daven was stomping about out there above a tunnel with unknown stability issues. She felt dirt drop on the back of her head and her calm shattered.

"Daven! Stop!"

There was one last beat, but it was followed by the sounds of a cave-in. The ground shifted below and Daven gave a quick yelp that was quickly drowned out by the noises inside. A dust cloud rose to meet her, choking the air. She took a deep gulp of air, covered her head with her arms and held very still as the rumbling subsided. She held still as long as her lungs could hold, and then exhaled loudly into the darkness. She coughed as she inhaled the dusty air.

"Daven?" she called out. There was no response and Kina's thoughts began to imagine the worst. Daven had likely caused the tunnel to collapse beneath his feet, and he would have been sucked down into the earth. She wriggled free of the rocky opening and reemerged into daylight. "Daven!" She hustled over the rocks, finding her footing across the uneven ground easily as she climbed to find the thief.

There was a good-sized hole in the ground which no doubt had been the point where Daven had been standing. She prayed to Veran silently that Daven was alright within before scrambling down to investigate. Half buried in the dirt below, but somehow standing upright, Daven looked up at her with an annoyed expression.

"Why does Fate curse me so?" His question, despite the lingering frustration in his voice, drew a smile on her lips. It seemed that despite Daven's claims to knowing little about ancient gods, he was clearly a believer. She left her observation to herself. Clearly unharmed, Daven drummed his fingers on the dirt pile that had swallowed his legs to his waist.

"You see this as a curse, clearly this is a blessing." She slid down purposefully into the hole and landed next to Daven softly. She looked down into the void with a pleased smile. "Definitely a blessing. The tunnel is intact."

"Great." Daven grumbled. "Get me out of here."

She looked to him and shrugged. "I'm going to have to dig you out with my hands," she warned him. "I will have to get pretty close."

"And?" Daven questioned, that maddening voice and sardonic smile brought to bear once more.

"So far you've kept your distance from me. I imagine my appearance does cause some discomfort."

"Look, being buried alive is somewhat uncomfortable. Being dug out by a young Fanerian woman makes it bearable."

"I have a tail," she noted, pointing at the offending appendage, while trying to ignore why Daven might have thought being helped by a young Fanerian girl would make his situation better.

"And you are needlessly concerned about it," Daven told her. "If your appearance truly bothered me, I would have left you behind." She grinned happily. He blinked at her. "How do you make those ears twitch like that?"

"Like what?" she asked.

"Like, well..." He put his hands next to his head and moved his fingers a bit, much to her amusement. "Never mind," he said at her giggling. He pushed at the dirt with his hands. "Just get me out of here."

She nodded, and moved next to him. On her knees, she began to pull the dirt away from him with her hands, taking armfuls away at a time. She didn't give herself any room to think of the awkwardness of her position. It seemed far too familiar to be touching him, but it was necessary to help free him.

Sensing her discomfort, or perhaps maybe hiding some of his own, Daven talked about his journey across Edan. He described various chases he led scouts on through the wilderness in order to escape and how he eluded capture through Faneria. Kina listened politely and asked questions of truthful interest about his adventures. She had journeyed further with Drago, however, somehow it seemed far more interesting to hear tales from Daven than it had to live similar events herself. She may have been a simple wanderer, but she recognized that Daven had both cunning and charisma to be a leader. She understood the differences between ruling through power and willingly following a leader.

"The look on his face," Daven laughed loudly, as Kina found herself trying to wipe the tears from her eyes with the back of a dirt smeared hand. "That poor man looked so angry that I thought he might drop dead right there. To this day I have no idea how I managed to have two different colored boots. I looked like a jester!"

Kina grinned and sat down heavily upon the loose dirt. "I wish I had the chance to visit one of the great Fanerian castles. They sound so wonderful."

"Depends of course," Daven told her as if weighing thoughts in his head. "It does not agree with all kinds. How about yourself? Surely you must have an interesting path for you to have learned so much. Who taught you about these ruins?"

Kina's smile faded slightly. "I had no teacher."

Daven looked at her, his own mirth balancing. "No, you must have had somebody teach you."

Kina's memories were not entirely pleasant. "I'm afraid my tale is somewhat less entertaining than your own."

"Kina, I am not going to think any less of you. I know enough to realize that the woman before me should not be defined by the company she has kept. You show intelligence that I have not seen often, and I have traveled many lands."

Kina shifted where she sat unhappily. "I left home at a young age, before my family could marry me off to another dismal life. I wandered for a while, scavenging for scraps. It was not a good life. When Drago found me, he offered me something no one else ever did. He gave me a chance to feel important. Drago had discovered a ruin, though nearly impassable by man. He had taken to collecting kids from the streets and sending them into the caverns with hopes they would return the treasure to him. Few survived long enough to return much of anything, but they must have told him about the treasures they had seen within.

"I listened carefully to the few warnings I was given, but nothing really prepared me for what I encountered underground. I came up twice without finding more than dead children. Each time, Drago sent me back into the hole without delay. Eventually, I stumbled upon the treasure room for which I was sent. I retraced my steps many times over the next few days. It became easier to just shut out everything and focus on the fact that I had done something none of the others before me had been able to achieve."

She watched him carefully, studying his expressions, and hoped to see some understanding. He remained unreadable to her, looking very serious. It made him look very different than how he generally appeared to her.

"I learned on my own," she told him firmly. "Drago knows of only treasure and power. To him a ruin means one thing, potential riches and gain. Over time I began to notice things within that were the same. Images, carvings, depictions of various peoples. Faded battle colors on banners so fragile that a mere breath would reduce them to dust. And I remembered everything and would puzzle the secrets alone at night. I would listen to the legends the elders told, and the songs that were sung." She looked about the interior of the tunnel as she tried to make Daven feel the wonder she held for such places now. "There are stories long forgotten. Things we should not have forgotten."

She found that Daven was looking at her in a studious manner that made her uneasy. She did not feel threatened by his gaze, but she felt that she had said too much and now he held some sort of power over her, knowing her intimate secrets as he now did.

At last he smirked, a look that made him all the more stunning. "I knew there was more to you than a simple knave."

She felt disappointed and insulted by his words. She had hoped for something more. He laughed at her, and she found herself meeting his expression angrily, despite wishing to leave.

"I'm sorry, I didn't mean that to be a slight," he told her with a smile. "You are a very intelligent woman, perhaps startlingly so, however, you really must allow yourself to learn about your curse. It is more telling of your emotions than any words you could say."

"Why?"

"While many people can hide their emotions but for their eyes, you will find, with those ears and tail, that you have become the most honest of people." Daven's smile saddened and she saw the shadows of his past haunt him once more. "Kina, tell me, what happened to the others?"

"The others?"

"The ones that came before you, that Drago sent into whatever hell he had found."

Kina shivered and wrapped her arms across her chest. Goosebumps raised on her skin, prickled as if touched by a cold wind. "They were butchered, killed in unspeakable ways. I remember them as well, the looks on their faces as they lay dead and cold upon the ground."

"Drago?"

"Wraiths."

She heard him inhale sharply. "I've heard talk of such things, but I thought they were legend."

"They are quite real, I assure you." Kina remembered them as well. "I've encountered them again since, and each time they have brought death in their wake. They have no physical form, but they can interact with our world when they wish it. Horrible, whispering things; the legends are tame in comparison."

Daven lowered his head and whispered a prayer that went mostly unheard by Kina. She recognized the passage, however, a reading for the dead as said by followers of the fallen Gods of Time. She found further comfort through Daven's shared faith and his mourning for those he had never met.

"And Drago sent them in to their fate." His voice was cold and hard, and she saw something more in his eyes now that frightened her.

She slid back in the dirt away from him. "Drago is not all that evil," Kina protested. "He paid me well for my services and protected me most of my life."

"He turned on you pretty quickly after you were cursed, didn't he?" Daven argued. "I know the type. You were of value to him and you were to be protected until that changed. Guess what, you became something of a liability when you became cursed. His interest in you is probably limited to that sword you carry. If he had that, he wouldn't have chased you from Brighton. You would already be dead to him."

"No."

"I will not argue. Think about it to yourself and you will come to your own answer." He wiggled his legs as much as he could within the mound and gave a good solid pull. His leg did not come free however. "When you are freed of your curse, do not go back to him. That would be your end."

He didn't give her time to think of his words then, instead he returned her focus upon freeing him. "I think I can just about get out, just a bit further." He leaned over and began to clear away the soil from his far leg, giving her room to help again. He didn't ask for her help, though it was implied that she had the choice to keep her distance. She wondered if that was intentional. Still, she once more moved close to him and worked rapidly to the completion of her task.

By the time they reached his knees, Daven was able to pull his legs free, though he lost a boot to the hole which rapidly filled in. Cursing, Daven stumbled back and fell on his seat. Dirty and tired, Kina laughed again at Daven. She silenced herself quickly for fear of drawing out his anger, but he showed no sign of it.

"Sure, laugh," he said instead. "I needed a new pair anyway." He removed the other one and poured out sand and stone unhappily. His pants were stained and damp from the ordeal, but remained untorn. She could feel the soil drying on her face and her hands were dark and stained. She could only wonder how dirty she must have appeared to Daven.

"Think the pond would work to clean up?"

"I think not. The bottom is soft. You would likely end up more muddied than you are now if you waded in. You could wash your hands and face from the edge." Daven's answer wasn't what she had hoped for. She looked at her pants and the sleeves of her shirt and shrugged. Dirty as they were, she was used to it.

"I don't believe we'll be going any further this night," she told Daven as she looked at the dark hole in the earth. "Tomorrow I want to find out what is down there."

"What if it's nothing?"

"Then I will take the knowledge that this is a true ruin in all meanings of the word."

Kina's ears noted Lyle's approach before he spoke. "What have you two been doing?" he asked as he looked down the hole at them. Kina looked to Daven, but noted the younger brother was laughing lightly to himself.

"Learning to be careful of where one steps," Daven replied

with good spirits.

"Wish you had learned that lesson long ago," Lyle muttered and turned to walk away.

"Not all can follow the guiding strings." Lyle made a disgusted noise and his footsteps faded away on the ground as he made his way back to his camp. Kina watched Daven as he leaned his head back against the wall of the tunnel.

"We may as well go back as well," Kina said, not wanting to further aggravate Lyle.

"And what would we do back there?"

Kina stood and brushed some of the drying dirt from her hands and clothing. "Well, you could tell me how you managed to burn down a castle." She looked across at him slyly as his head came up sharply to look at her. She turned to take in his gaze with a triumphant smile. "I remember everything, I said. Lyle mentioned it back at Ishaw."

Daven blinked in surprise, and then again. "I wish you would stop making your ears do that."

"Do what?"

"Never mind."

When they returned to camp, Lyle was waiting for them at the tree, a fire burning brightly in the well used pit. Kina gazed at the fire, thankful for the warmth after spending time underground. She cast a glance at Daven and noted that he sat closer to the fire, huddled up as if cold and silently thinking. She waited patiently for him, listening to the crackle of the fire and the singing of nature's night. The sound of a hopper reminded her of the meal she had shared with Daven in the field. She had not eaten much since and suddenly she felt the pains of hunger as if remembering had triggered the response. Uncomfortable now, she shifted restlessly.

"You keep fidgeting like that and I will toss you in the pond," Lyle told her gruffly from where he had been quietly brooding.

She sent him a sharp glare which she softened for fear that he was serious.

"As you will," she told him submissively.

"Lyle, stop it," Daven ordered in a firm tone he had yet to take with his brother.

"And what would you do to prevent me?"

Daven looked up and glared for a moment before flashing a smile that contained much strangeness. "On second thought, perhaps I should let you do as you will. You are proving me to be the good Hitchcliffe while you take the role of the villain."

"And what is that supposed to mean?"

"It means you are being unreasonable." Daven shrugged and brushed at some of the dried dirt on his pants without concern. "Not that that should be any surprise. What have you to eat?"

"Food?" Lyle grumped, sending Daven an angered look. "You expect me to share my food with a criminal?"

"Well, when you put it that way..." Daven got up and stretched. Kina watched him with interest, wondering why he had given in so easily. It was much to her surprise then that Daven made his way casually to Lyle's bag and began digging through it. Lyle said nothing, instead turning his attention to her.

"I suppose you are like him," he ventured. "A thief and a criminal."

"No," she protested, denying the fact that she had stolen a horse in her escape and killed Loor.

"Then what is it you do? Clearly, you do not stay at home and tend to village children."

"I find things," Kina answered, smiling fondly at Daven as he chewed on something he had taken from Lyle. "Treasures and magical items."

"And trouble," Lyle remarked. While she didn't answer, she couldn't help but agree with him. She was surprised by Lyle's apparent acceptance of her answer, however, as he grumbled to himself without further questions or even looking curious. She was almost disappointed that she could be so uninteresting to him.

The following morning, Kina was awakened just before dawn by the quiet efforts of two experienced travelers packing up their camp. She blinked away her dreams and watched as Daven and Lyle seemed to work as one, efficiently loading up the two horses without argument. She yawned loudly, drawing Daven's attention only briefly. He flashed her one of his arrogant-looking grins while trying to roll up a blanket tight enough to fit into a travel bag.

Curiosity got the better of her, and she spoke first. "What's the matter?"

"Nothing much," Daven answered, succeeding with a bit of effort to shove the blanket inside the bag. "Lyle and I decided it was best if we started out early."

"Oh," she replied. Her mind took a moment to circle back to her own plans for the day. "But I wanted to explore that tunnel you found."

Daven paused with a heavy sigh. He looked her way and then back over his shoulder at Lyle. The bigger man snorted darkly, a sound that seemed to say that he was too important to be delayed by her curiosity. Daven looked back at her and shrugged unhelpfully.

"We really need to find a mage. I don't think there are any down that hole."

Kina tossed the blanket off and quickly began to ready herself. She strapped the sword back to her side and stood tall. If they wanted to leave her behind, they would not go far without the sword. She stretched out the morning stiffness from her body as she considered what she was about to do. The old her would have silently accepted their decision. Now, though still tempted to do so, she thought about doing what she wanted.

"Where are we going?" she asked, fighting the impulsive thoughts in her head.

"South," Daven answered simply. "I know you wanted to go to Brighton, but if your ancient race was last seen on the coast, we might find out more there. Besides, the further we get from the Duke, the better."

She nodded, accepting the decision. "Fine. But I'm not leaving yet," she replied. She was surprised by the firmness of her own voice. Lyle and Daven both stopped loading up the horses to look at her through the shadows of dawn. "Please?" she asked, hoping they wouldn't just drag her along with them by force.

Lyle cast his hands into the air, cursing loudly. "Of course," he muttered when his voice became intelligible once more. "Why not just ask for the Duke to come get us?"

"Midday," Daven said, ignoring his brother. "We shouldn't stay here any longer than that."

"That will be fine," she returned, smilingly happily. "Thank you!"

"Yes, yes," Daven returned, waving his hands to deflect her thanks. "Lyle, can you handle the rest yourself?"

Lyle glared at Daven in response.

"Right, of course you can." Looking at her, Daven tossed the bag he was packing aside. "Let's be off."

Lit by the light of a fresh torch, the old tunnel looked uncomfortably unstable to Kina. The stone blocks had shifted over time, collapsing parts of the tunnel and making passage difficult in most other places. The floor was uneven, and the walls looked as though they were ready to spill into the passage.

Yet, despite her discomfort, she recognized the familiar feelings the cavern gave her. This was old, she decided confidently. It was easily as old as the temple she had found near Brighton. The ancient stones had probably not been touched by sentient life in generations. She wondered what the last people had thought when they had walked through these tunnels.

"Kina, are you sure about this?" Daven was behind her, stumbling over nearly every upturned stone without his boots. "The cave is probably blocked anyway."

"If it's blocked, then we will find out soon enough," Kina replied, lowering herself to duck beneath a large stone that had fallen diagonally across the tunnel. She quietly hoped that this ruin had not been completely lost to time. She wanted to find something to validate herself to Daven and Lyle both. If all she found was a pile of broken rock, then she would lose what little bit of credence she had built.

"It's unusual to find a ruin like this," Kina admitted to Daven as she stood up again afterward. "Normally, I have folktales and legends that need to be sorted through and mapped. To find a ruin on the surface normally means that it will have been looted of anything valuable ages before. Sometimes those who plundered them will have caused further destruction within, removing all traces of who built them." Kina hesitated before a particularly uneven stretch ahead. It looked firm enough, however, so she continued with care. "I'm hoping that the entrance way collapsed shortly after the place was abandoned. That would prevent any looters from getting access to the main chambers and rooms within."

"Why did these ancients have to build everything underground?"

Kina paused and looked at the walls carefully. She considered the shape and structure and compared it to what she knew of modern construction techniques. While she had never set foot in a full castle, she had been in numerous temples and even some of the old border forts. Closing her eyes, she pictured the other ruins she had explored, and noted the similarities and differences of each.

"Not everything they built was meant to be underground," she said with certainty that was near absolute. "I think over time they have been buried and forgotten. This one, however... I think it is supposed to be underground. The construction techniques seem similar to that of some of the crypts beneath the temples of Ganodu."

"Isn't that the name of the God of Life?"

"I'm impressed. Not many care to learn the proper names."

"I'm afraid I never understood this particular custom. Why bury their dead beneath the temple of Life?"

Kina grinned morbidly at Daven's comment. "I think they believe that by bringing their dead to Ganodu, the spirit of their loved ones will live on forever." She shrugged and continued her way deeper into the tunnels. "Really, it's not that hard to understand why they would want to believe that. That's why the Gods of Light are so popular. They promise nothing but gifts and speak nothing of costs. Pardon me if I... Oh." She looked over her shoulder at Daven briefly, noting his look of amusement, and tried to focus on the path ahead of her. "Forgive me, I shouldn't speak that way. Sometimes I forget myself."

"I'm not insulted in the slightest," Daven responded. "You seem to know a good deal for somebody that does not believe."

Kina coughed, covering any sort of audible reaction to Daven's observation, incorrect as it was. "Folklore and legends," she responded when she felt that she had enough control back to answer without giving away too much. One didn't advertise that they worshiped the old gods, even to those suspected of having similar leanings.

"It's something more than that," Daven noted.

"I remember everything," she told Daven again. "And I have been in many places that few have been allowed to journey. Of course I sound knowledgeable about these things."

"Not it," he replied confidently. "But I understand that it's not something I need to know of you." She breathed with relief and tried to concentrate on the uneven path before her. Daven's torch illuminated a misshapen mass ahead of her, but darkly recognizable to her experienced eyes. Bones. Old, but certainly human looking. Sure enough, as she approached she could see the broken skull laying near the wall. There was a hole in the side of the head, and somehow she doubted it was caused by anything after death. She hesitated warily and gazed about the tunnel for signs of danger.

Daven waited behind her, but he was unable to see the broken skeleton. "What is it?" He didn't sound alarmed, but they both knew this was more her element than his.

She didn't say anything. She approached the body slowly, ever alert for signs of danger. The bones were very old, making it unlikely that whatever had killed this man was still present, but she wouldn't bet her life on that assumption. The remains of old clothing lay in small tattered shapes amidst the dust and dirt, as did a broken sword. The hilt lay across the man's lap as though he had held onto it into death. She looked about the corridor, gazing at the walls, the floor, the ceiling, looking for signs to what had happened here. She was not a tracker, however, and she needed more than subtle hints in the dirt to tell her this man's story.

Glancing over her shoulder at Daven briefly, she returned her gaze to the fallen momentarily. She closed her eyes and silently whispered prayers over the body, aware that Daven would likely guess what she was doing. Still, she would not risk falling further from favor just to hide her beliefs.

"He died fighting," Daven noted, leaning close to her to peer upon the body. "Blunt force to the head."

She looked at him in surprise at his observation. "You can read the signs?"

"Not fully, but I know war. The breaks suggest he was hit, and the broken sword suggests he knew of danger. Beyond that, I could not say how he came to his fate. It is enough to know that he died long before we found this hole."

Kina nodded, and stepped around the skeleton. There was nothing more to learn from this one. Unfortunately, it would soon seem that he had not died alone. They encountered another two ancient bodies strewn over the floor, each showing signs of falling in battle.

"Strange that they have no belongings," Daven noted.

Kina bit her lip. It was not strange to her, though it was not a welcome thought. "Somebody has been here since." She thought of the jumbled skeletons and reconsidered. "No, then the bones would have been scattered. Somebody took from them not long after their passing."

"Right," Daven agreed, though his tone was cool. "But who were they?"

"I want to know what this place was," Kina answered. The mysteries she was discovering only fueled her determination. "We find out that, and we may find out who these people were and who attacked them." She moved with a bit more haste now, aware that midday was approaching and soon Daven would force her to turn back. It wasn't much further to the end of the tunnel, however, and soon the light of his torch illuminated a solemn room barren of writing. There were more dead here. As many as five or six had fallen during some ancient battle. It appeared as though anything of value had been carried away long ago, leaving the dead where they lay. What looked to be an altar stood in the center of the room, made of stone apparently carved from the earth.

"Ganodu," Daven said, believing that the ruin must have belonged to the God of Life.

"No," she disagreed. "There are no crypts here. This place was never meant to house the dead." She looked at the bones again sadly. It was quite apparent that despite the purpose of this place, that was indeed what it became. "Strange that there are no murals, or writings. Temples are generally decorated well."

"Somebody took everything else out, why not…" His voice drifted off uncertainly. Kina looked to him and noted the strange expression that had taken root on his face. "I don't think we should be here."

"Why, what is it?"

"The shadows," Daven noted as he backed up carefully toward the entrance. "They move."

Icy fingers gripped her soul. She looked about, never allowing her eyes to remain upon any one spot for more than a heartbeat. She could hear scratchy whispers now, sounds she had come to recognize as wraiths. A sound much like a knife on stone. Whatever this place was, it was not welcoming to those of the living.

She saw glimpses of the movement and edged closer to the exit herself. These were not wraiths, but she doubted that they would be any less deadly. As one, the shadows stepped forward, illuminating themselves with their own inner light. The ghostly apparitions moved forward menacingly, images Kina realized of men long dead to this world. There were a dozen of them, if not more hidden in shadow, and they were armed. Swords and armor adorned the dead as though they were about to do battle.

"For uncountable years we have slept," said one that stood a stride closer than any of the others. Kina noted that while he glanced at Daven occasionally, his attention was primarily for her. "Our cursed sleep for failing our duty to defend this temple has not been disturbed once till now for fear of our wrath. You who sealed us away return now to face our justice."

"We can leave, and you can go back to sleep." Daven spoke with strange calm, offering an implausible solution to their problem.

Kina had no doubt that these ghosts would attack if she fled, so she chose an alternate path. Spirits and ghosts were linked to this world through their own lives, but where spirits were benign, ghosts were known to hold something of a grudge. That link to their former lives, however, could sometimes be used to reason with them. At least, that was what she had been told by a scant few who said they had done so. They were not overly powerful, but they could be dangerous if taken lightly.

"We didn't mean to intrude upon your sacred ground," she said diplomatically, inclining her head ever so slightly. "I'm afraid you are mistaken, we had no part in your deaths."

"The sword you carry betrays you," the ghost snarled, aggression showing through the deteriorated facial features. "The Blade of Vashnir was stolen during the attack. The weapon gives way your true allegiance."

Kina's mind held anything she could say silent while she tried to link the name to anything she knew. She grasped at a memory of an old man who claimed to have once been a spirit guide. He had spoken of the sword named such belonging to a demi-goddess in the times before. It had been Nephrita, patron of chaos, who had been the owner of Vashnir. A name connected to Veran quite closely. Daughter of change, bringer of chaos.

She slid the sword from its sheath at her side and looked upon it with new-found curiosity. "This sword belonged to Nephrita?" Kina asked. "How did it come to be here?"

"We brought it here," the ghost declared, as if daring her to argue otherwise. She decided it was probably not in her best interest, besides, it was entirely possible that these ghosts had lived during the Time of Gods and Magic. "And here it will remain."

She twitched, and looked away from the sword to meet the eyeless face of the ghost. "Not until I undo the curse it has laid upon me." Behind her, she could hear Daven pulling out a weapon of his own, though she could hardly blame him. The menace in the room was almost physical, and she doubted it would be long until it came to a fight. If the sword had indeed belonged to Nephrita, then it was likely she was standing within an old temple to the God of Strength, Annasus. "This is a temple to Annasus, is it not? Where are the tributes? Where are the banners to your patron god?"

"Stolen, by those like you lured by the dark promises of the fallen."

"I see," Kina answered. This was not going to be pleasant. Annasus, unlike what was preached in his modern temples, was storied to be an unpleasant character and many of his early followers had been likewise unlikable. She glanced at Daven and noted that he was quite prepared to charge into a battle he couldn't win. She needed to keep talking. If they continued talking it would delay any fighting, whether instigated by ghosts or Daven. "I assure you we share no connection to those who destroyed your temple. We only search for a cure to my curse. If you will not help, then we shall leave you in peace."

"You will never leave this temple," the ghost told her. A ghastly smile spread on his tortured features.

She looked hard at the ghost, showing none of the fear she felt within. She had learned enough from the short conversation with the ghosts to threaten them back. If they believed her bluff, she and Daven would have time to escape. She forced a grin onto her face and stared hard at the dead. "If you make any attack upon me or my friend, you will regret it. Your anonymous gods have forsaken these lands and no longer feel need to help their followers. The power of Veran becomes strong once more." She lifted the sword before her and gripped it with both hands to keep it steady. "I believe Veran would be most displeased with the fate of her favored offspring, and those who further speak ill of her. Begone! Begone and allow us to leave here in peace!"

The sword surged with power, surprising all within the

forgotten temple, none more than Kina herself. It shone with an unnatural light that threatened to blind her eyes. Perhaps this really was Vashnir in her possession. Through the cries of the ghosts, Kina realized she had her moment of distraction. It was time to go. She turned and raced for the exit, grabbing Daven's arm as she ran past him and leading him back into the tunnel.

"Nice trick!" he yelled over her shoulder.

"I had little part in it," she returned back just as loudly. The cries of the dead were fast becoming screams of rage and she doubted they had much time before they would begin to give chase. "It would appear that by invoking Veran's name that I may have brought on some divine intervention."

"Who is Veran?" Daven's voice hinted his frustration through his tone.

"The Goddess of Change."

"Are you saying one of the old gods answered your call inside the temple of a God of the Light?"

"From the stories, Veran remained free. Seemed like a good idea at the time."

"I thought the Gods of Time had no power in this land."

"Who is to say otherwise?" The screams were getting quieter, though no less intense. It would appear that whatever kept them from crossing over also kept the ghosts of the dead imprisoned within the main chamber. An interesting curse, and very lucky for her. "Worship of them is just about forbidden by the ruling kings."

"Kina," Daven grunted as he pushed his way through a narrow stretch, "who is Nephrita?"

"Fallen demi-goddess," she responded, connecting more incomplete stories. "I believe defeated during the Time of Gods and Magic by Annasus, God of Strength."

"I think what we have seen here gives weight to that story," Daven snorted. "None of this tells me who Nephrita was though."

"The old gods sired many children in this land, so it is told. Nephrita was said to be the eldest of Veran's three daughters. She became the patron of Chaos sometime later. Impulsive would be the best word I could use to describe what I have heard." The other two, Laural and Petra, were less well known but even what was written about them suggested that Nephrita was something of an oddity in that she had power that rivaled that of the true blooded gods.

"I hadn't heard of children of the gods before. She must have been very impulsive indeed to take on the God of Strength."

"Or very powerful," Kina corrected. "In either event, she was imprisoned by the Gods of Light. Apparently Annasus liked to take trophies. If what we just heard is true, Annasus brought Vashnir to his temple before he left this world. Somebody else decided they wanted it enough to destroy his temple."

"So much for your ancient race."

"Perhaps. It still could have been them who raided this place. If this is the true sword of Nephrita, and I believe that it is, then we could focus on finding some of the old temples."

"More holes to crawl through," Daven remarked none too brightly.

Kina wasn't so certain. There were questions to be answered. She needed to speak with someone knowledgeable on the old gods, which again led her further away from Brighton. Temples to the Gods of Time were few since the Time of Gods and Magic. The Light Gods and their followers had destroyed most of them, and many that remained were located far to the east.

Despite this, she still felt the lingering doubts. Brighton was still key, but she could not explain why she felt this. What had that temple been in the times of old? Why had a person of such power been buried with Vashnir, the sword of a deposed goddess?

Most concerning was she now felt some of the fear that Lyle and Daven had shared. Why did Duke Gawthrain want a sword belonging to the patron of Chaos? The Duke could not be allowed to get his hands on it, she agreed, but she knew now that they would be hunted beyond the borders of the Duke's influence. She would not be safe anywhere she traveled within Edan. She doubted the borders of Faneria would offer her much sanctuary while she still held Vashnir.

When they reached the entrance way to the tunnel, Lyle was waiting for them just outside. He must have heard their approach because he shifted slightly and looked about. From where Kina and Daven stood inside the tunnel, it appeared that Lyle was trying not to look into the hole at them.

"Stay down," he told them, his voice sounding calm but quiet, and he still did not turn to face them. Kina fidgeted restlessly and stared back down the dark passage. It wasn't comforting thinking of the ghosts that remained inside, but at least she was fairly certain they were not coming after her at this point. She couldn't even hear their cries of rage any longer.

"What is it?" Daven whispered. Kina noted he had put his hand on his sword.

"I just had a visit from some of the Duke's men. They seemed satisfied to leave me be, but they could still be near. Just stay down there for now." Lyle threw a stone into the hole, and Kina watched it bounce along the ground. "We might best stay here another night."

It was still fairly early in the day and Lyle's comment caught her by surprise. She looked to Daven, who seemed to be considering it. "It could be a good idea. They give you any trouble about the horse?"

"Should they have?"

"Only if they were looking carefully."

"They knew I was from Faneria, but asked only what I had seen. Somebody is pressing them pretty hard to find you. We will need to be more careful."

Daven looked at Kina with some concern evident on his face. "I would rather start moving," he told her and his brother alike. "They will have to return once they realize they have lost our trail. I would like to put a couple of days' worth of travel before we stop again."

Kina opened her mouth to protest but just as quickly closed it again. As much as she wanted to learn more about this temple and its connections to the sword she carried, perhaps Daven was right and they needed to first make sure that Vashnir was safe from the Duke.

Chapter Five

They traveled for long hours at a time, pausing only for the briefest of rests, as they sought to put distance between Vashnir and Brighton. While the two brothers found her new sense of urgency odd, they did not ask why Kina felt they needed to travel quickly. She wondered if they had already realized the dangers themselves. They discussed the best paths to avoid scouts and she discovered a topic which the two did not argue upon. She could see their shared experience and training as they discussed and often agreed upon trails that seemed no different to her eyes. They still argued, often in fact, but Kina noted that they seemed comfortable in each other's presence.

Occasionally, they would be forced to go into town for supplies. She quickly became aware of the signs before either would speak the need. There was a tension that would be present in their faces and they would become much more cautious about where they led her. Eventually, they would tell her of their need and ask her what information she needed in town. One of the two brothers would ride into town and ask her questions and return with the mostly unhelpful answers. The supplies they needed were bought or bartered for with what little they had. Daven returned from the first town with a new pair of boots, though they looked expensive and slightly used. She didn't know how the brothers stretched what little money they had, but there was always something edible to eat. Often she wished there wasn't, as some of the supplied meals tasted worse than the hopper meat Daven had introduced her to. The nights when food was caught fresh were often much happier.

Kina was happy to be traveling with good company, but she wished she were allowed to go to town. There were questions they just could not ask. Recognizing that there were dangers involved kept her from pressing the issue too hard. More than once, she would be hurried away by the remaining brother as the Duke's scouts were sighted in the distance. Kina learned very quickly that the two both had great respect for the tracking scouts, and that they preferred to keep their distance rather than trust their luck with subtle tricks.

When alone with Daven, she found she spent time listening to his outrageous tales. He had even taken to teaching her how to use a sword, though it quickly became apparent that she was hopeless at fighting with one. She may have had plenty of balance, but she lacked in physical strength and she flinched away from any blow sent in her direction. Daven didn't appear discouraged, but she expected that he was continuing with the lessons only to pass the time.

When it was Daven's turn to go into town, she found herself resting with Lyle. The elder brother rarely spoke much at all, and she found that she too fell into habitual silence when left alone with him. She was left with the impression that he disliked the position in which she had put him. It always seemed that Lyle was watching her from the corner of his eye, never letting her stray far from sight. When she thought about it, she could hardly blame him. She had lived in the darker side of life after all, as she had been living with one of the most dangerous men in the region. No doubt he viewed her as tainted, and she couldn't argue otherwise. So she accepted the quiet, answered any questions Lyle had for her and asked none of her own.

Every day she was shepherded further from Brighton and the secrets she had uncovered. Every day, she felt, she was taken further from the answers she sought. Kina stood at the edge of the tree line, gazing back in the direction of Brighton. She had never been to this part of Edan before, but she knew exactly where the great castle lay. Behind her she could hear Daven approaching, but she allowed him to come up behind her.

"You haven't said a word in over a day," he said simply. She considered keeping her feelings to herself. She was already such a burden on the pair. Yet Daven, of all people, deserved to have a truthful answer.

"I know in my head that we must go," she answered at last, "but I cannot help but feel that I must return. I don't understand."

Daven's arms gripped her shoulders and with firm but gentle pressure turned her round to face him. He smiled, but his eyes were sad. "You lost a lot in Brighton, Kina. Naturally you feel the need to return and try to pick up the pieces. I will tell you, there is nothing left for you there."

She looked away from his eyes, finding interest in the grass growing at the foot of the tree. Searching her feelings, she had to disagree with Daven. It wasn't her life she was mourning. "I don't think that's it," she returned. "I have that feeling of loss, but more still I feel a calling. A whisper tugging at my every thought."

"Maybe you can hear something with those ears," Daven responded, a sly grin spreading on his features.

"Not funny."

"The voice of truth?"

Anger rose within her and she shoved his arms from her violently. "Stop it."

"Your ears went flat," Daven commented, smirking at her. "You realize that there are several hundred armed men between you and that castle now, of course. Who knows whether or not your friend Drago is among them? You have half the kingdom looking for you, trying to cash in on the reward posted for your capture, and you want to head back to Brighton?"

Kina patted her hair around her ears, a poor attempt to hide her frustration. Daven's response to her honesty surprised her and left her feeling angry and embarrassed. "I didn't say I wanted to go back," she told Daven, biting back the urge to strike out verbally. "I said I felt I need to go back."

"You say you remember everything," Daven commented, his smile slipping as he became serious once more, "remember this. I will stay by your side for as long as it takes. There is no need to rush back and get yourself killed."

She felt her face warm, and she looked away from him again. Daven confused her like no other had in her lifetime. Nothing Kina had learned in her life about dealing with people prepared her for the ever shifting moods he caused within her. She found herself facing in the direction of Brighton without meaning to.

"I need to do something," she said sheepishly. "You and Lyle do so much for me."

"Give it time. You seem to be the expert in old relics, so you will have to rely on yourself for the answers you seek." Daven snickered. "Best Lyle could come up with is for you to just get used to your new features."

Kina sighed, her body slumping as she allowed herself a moment of self-pity. She had made remarkable progress in discovering the history of the sword, but despite all she knew, she was no closer to finding out why it had transformed her.

She looked out into the distance. "What if I have to spend the rest of my life like this?" Trapped within her own body, forced to look upon the world from a distance. "I don't have the strength to live my life like this," she said, hoping that Daven would have an answer that would give her strength.

She jerked as she felt his hands grasp her tail, and she whirled to face him, tearing her appendage from his grip with the motion. Despite her glare, Daven merely grinned and shrugged. "You have plenty of strength. Just keep moving. We will find a mage who can cure you soon."

"I can already guess what you would like once that day comes," she snapped at him. "It will take more than your smile to bed me."

Eyebrows raised, Daven's maddening smirk grew. "I guess I have until that day to figure out what it will take, then." He turned and walked away, leaving Kina feeling scandalized and embarrassed.

She rode out the wave of emotions before looking back over the horizon. A reluctant smile spread across her lips as she wrapped her arms around herself. "I hope I don't have to wait long," she sighed.

It was three days later when they got their first break. Daven picked up a rumor from a trading caravan that there was a mage seen in recent times within a small town by the name of Renoa. It surprised her, but Daven and Lyle agreed she should go into town with them. It was their first good lead on any kind of magic in this land, so it seemed neither of the two brothers wanted to waste an opportunity.

The journey seemed long to Kina despite her knowledge that they had already traveled much further and harder to this point. She knew also it was only the anticipation that was causing this illusion. Knowing, however, didn't allow her to completely remove herself from the feeling that this leg of her journey was the longest.

The trio received a reminder that they were still being hunted early on the second morning. Four horseback mounted soldiers rode hard past their camp. Had they chosen a more open position, Kina had little doubt that they would have been seen. Daven fell behind as Lyle rushed Kina away from camp, once more covered in Daven's old cloak. She learned later that Daven had spent several hours masking their tracks so that the Duke's scouts would not track them so easily should they circle back. That was a trick she wanted to learn, but was one secret that Daven did not divulge. The look in Lyle's eyes suggested that perhaps the younger brother had done more than just hide their their passage.

Kina played with the hood on her cloak timidly while she waited at the table. Lyle was out trying to find supplies in town using the last of her coins and a few more volunteered by Daven. Daven was asking the innkeeper for information about magic, while she tried her best to eat her meal without being obvious. Shrouded in her cloak, Kina tried to avoid fidgeting with the heavy fabric. She would have much preferred to be allowed to mingle and ask questions of the locals, but she wasn't going to complain.

From where she sat, she could tell that Daven wasn't getting the answers he needed. The subtle changes in Daven's expression as the innkeeper shook his head in the negative, the body language displayed when the innkeeper spoke, all seemed to indicate that this town had been another waste of time. She made herself appear occupied by her plate when Daven turned away from the innkeeper.

Daven sat down heavily across from her at the table and gazed darkly at the streets through the open window. Kina chewed her last mouthful of potato thoughtfully while she considered how best to approach the subject.

Daven volunteered, however, without being prompted. "He hasn't heard of any magic users in these parts. As near as he can tell, there never has been a mage in Edan, but he strikes me as something of a devout worshiper of Life. Never can trust those folks."

Kina looked at Daven, unsure of his mood. "I have never heard that before. Why can you not trust them?"

Daven's grin was strangely dark. "They tend to get blinded by their own lives and what directly affects them. Only the devout."

"That is a pretty large generalization," she commented. "If you are so free with generalizations, what would you say about me?"

Daven's surprise was momentary. The confused look quickly melted into a strange sort of understanding. "I would say that you are the avatar of Veran." Despite the smile that appeared on his face, his words put Kina at ill ease. She slid back into her seat away from her plate warily.

"You invoke that name pretty lightly for having only heard me speak it once."

Daven was not so easily dissuaded and he seemed pretty excited by his observation. "Think about it, Kina. You seek change. You have changed. You are causing change in this land."

"Me?" Kina looked about uncertainly at the others within the tavern, touching the hood of her cloak to make sure it was still in place. Nobody seemed to care about them as they enjoyed the moment of food and relaxation with friends and kindred spirits.

"Well, it's possible." Daven shrugged as though it didn't matter, the intensity of his focus vanishing with the moment. "I suppose it is only fair that I tell you I am an equally ostracized follower of Fate. Had you guessed that I shared your devotion to the Gods of Time?"

For a moment, she felt a wave of warmth run through her as Daven finally trusted her enough to tell her. The moment didn't last though, and Kina twitched as she realized that his words were no longer for her to hear alone. Someone else approached, and Daven hadn't noticed.

"Perhaps it is time, young man," an older, gravelly voice grumbled softly, "that you remember why you are here." Daven turned abruptly and stared at the old man as Kina's eyes traveled to him as well. The white-haired man stood with a slight lean but looked strong. The dagger and large pouch on his belt suggested he did fairly well for himself in his old age, though the semi-vacant look to his eyes told another story. "And most importantly where here is, my boy."

"So noted," Daven answered, grinning. "And who might you be?"

"Just an old man," he answered with a dark grin. His head tracked upon Daven, but his eyes didn't seem to see him. "But, I am an old man who has seen a lot in his days."

"Your days were a long time ago it seems, old man," Daven remarked. "But I am willing to listen."

"Indeed. First, my own curiosity." The man turned and looked at Kina. She noted his eyes were dark, almost as dark as night. "Who might this lovely lady be, so maligned by the fallen gods?"

Kina didn't trust the friendly tones he struck with her. "Kina," she answered tentatively, unwilling to provide any more information.

Even blind it seemed the old man picked up on her mood. "No need to be nervous, my dear. I did not intend to listen in. Though from what I heard, you are looking for somebody who dabbles a bit in magic."

Kina felt a flicker of hope ignite within her and noted that Daven's posture seemed to straighten as well.

"You?" Daven asked, though he seemed to be asking a question that they all knew would be untrue.

"No, sadly not," the old man answered, shaking his head. "May I sit? These old bones are sore."

"There's a free chair to your right," Daven answered. "Need me to get it for you?"

The stranger scowled, and he pointed a crooked finger at Daven's face. "Appearances are deceiving. Just because I cannot see with my eyes does not mean I do not see what is around me." The man's hand reached out and pulled the chair away from the table without fumbling for the back. He moved effortlessly and sat, leaving Kina awestruck by how he moved without the benefit of eyesight.

"I apologize," Daven replied, nodding politely.

"I know what you thought you knew," the stranger growled. "You would be wise to cut your stay in Renoa short. Word travels that the Duke has taken interest in your companion." The man's eyes traveled across the table to Kina's own. "Young Ukiel."

Kina swallowed hard, fearing what else might be known of her.

"The Duke has interest in us?" Daven asked, his tone sounding more amused than frightened. "We are mere peddlers, but perhaps the Duke is a collector of shiny pebbles too?" At least it seemed to Kina that Daven was unaffected by the revelations.

The stranger regarded Daven a hard moment before breathing out in a muted laugh. "You are an odd one." The man's posture seemed to change and he returned his sightless gaze to Kina. "You seek magic. This is a land that fears such unworldly powers. Why do you risk yourself?"

Daven spoke up on Kina's behalf, saving her from her doubts. "Because we do not fear it. It would seem that neither do you."

"Indeed," the old man replied, again flashing more of a smile now. "I have seen enough in my time to know that the various magics in this land are as much part of nature as the birds and the trees."

Kina's mind grasped the implications of his words even as he spoke them. "You have encountered magic users before. Where?"

"Here and there." He paused and seemed to look out the window, though she realized what he saw was in the past. "Most were chased from these lands many years ago. Those that remain mostly stay to themselves. They tend to want to be left alone."

"You know where they are?" Kina pressed, eager for the knowledge.

The old man lowered his head and leaned back with a heavy

sigh. "You ask for which I cannot provide an easy answer. There are many schools of magic, my dear. A sorcerer, for instance, would not be able to provide the same help as, say, an enchanter. My question, that you have so carefully been trying to elude, is as important and valid as your own. Why do you seek magic?" A strange smile curled at the edge of one side of his mouth. "Would it happen to do with a certain sword stolen from Brighton?"

Even Daven looked uneasy at these words. "How did you hear of that?"

"Messenger arrived from Brighton yesterday. He posted a reward for the capture of young Ukiel before moving on. The sum of the reward outweighed the crimes, and further rumors from others coming from Brighton seemed to suggest that a sword was stolen during a meeting between Lord Gawthrain and a mercenary by the name of Drago Kramoris. You have escaped notice so far, but be warned: there are eyes searching for the young woman with magical powers to disguise herself." He chuckled lightly while Daven and Kina remained uncomfortably silent. "Had you magic to disguise yourself, Miss Ukiel, you would not cover yourself in such material."

Daven cleared his throat and looked at Kina carefully. His eyes seemed to suggest that she be quiet for the moment, and she was only too happy to do so. "If the rumors were true, and there was a magic sword involved, where would one look for answers?"

The old man closed his eyes and stroked the stubble on his chin as he grumbled to himself with a sound deep within his throat. "I know of one who may be able to help you," the old man said, though not sounding certain with his own thoughts. "Located within the walls of an old temple complex several days travel south from here there is an expert, as it were, on various enchantments and magical items. I happen to know there are none in Edan with knowledge rivaling this person."

"I think I know the place. Near Teleri. There is a catch, of course," Daven stated as he too noted the tone.

"Of course. I will say that this is not a generous soul, and I will say no more on the subject."

"Why?" Kina asked.

"What are you afraid of, old man?"

"While I may not fear magic itself, I am not without respect for the users of such magic. It is wise to treat some with a great deal of care. I will say that it has been long rumored that this person is no friend to the Duke of Deverell." The old man rose and seemed to look about the tavern warily. Had it not been for the eyes, Kina would have believed he was looking for somebody. "I do hope we meet again," the man stated, favoring her with a creepy looking smile.

Daven shrugged, a gesture that probably went unnoticed. "If that is our fate, perhaps someday we will cross paths. I do hope that we meet on good terms."

The smirk that appeared on the old man's face reminded Kina of Daven's own look of dark amusement. "When that day comes, fear not of me." The man stretched, nodding once to Kina, and began walking easily across the floor to the bar keep. Kina watched him go, noting that he also drew looks from the locals.

"Interesting," Daven commented, as he lounged in his chair. "One wonders how a blind man hears of a mage that none else would speak of."

"Among other wonders," Kina added uncomfortably.

"Learning to be more cautious of people?"

"Perhaps," Kina admitted. "How did he know who I was?"

"I suppose his hearing is good for his age," Daven grumbled, and looked over his shoulder. From his posture, Kina wondered if Daven too was concerned. "We have spoken too freely. Perhaps we should take his advice and leave Renoa behind us."

Kina would have it no other way. They knew where to find a mage at last, and she was mere days from reaching a potential cure.

*   *   *

As night began to fall some two days from Renoa, Kina allowed herself a moment to think beyond a cure. They were making great time across the dry, grassy plains of Edan, and not another soul had been seen. It had been three days since they had last seen signs of the Duke's scouts, which seemed to improve even Lyle's spirit. It seemed that at long last she was waking up from a bad dream.

The question was, what would she do once cured? If anything, these past weeks had shown her that she did not belong with Drago. As much as she desired his strength and comfort, she knew that there were those in the world that had those same traits and yet the kindness that she also longed for.

Kina started as she realized she had been staring at Daven, and looked away in embarrassment. She hoped the thief had not noticed her gaze. As luck would have it, he hadn't. His attention focused instead on unloading the horses of their burdens for the night. She thought of her more wild fantasies since coming to know him and wondered if he would allow her to stay by his side once their quest was completed. Watching him as he tossed the bedrolls on the ground, she found strange comfort in the hopes that he would.

Her eyes traveled to the safety of the night sky, and she tried to focus her thoughts upon the distant shining stars.

"You look happy," Daven noted, finally taking notice of her. "Your ears are up." Kina grinned and looked at him, gladly taking the invitation to join him in conversation.

"Hmmph," Lyle added. His tone had not changed, but Kina knew it wasn't her that had drawn the disapproval from the elder brother. She ignored him, much like Daven had.

"I was just thinking about what I'm going to do first when the curse is lifted."

"My guess would be to leap with joy," Daven commented with

a sly smile. She scowled at him, and he raised his hands in mock surrender.

"Honestly," she said, trying to make Daven see that she was serious. "My entire life I have spent looking for meaning. I thought I found myself searching the ruins of these lands, but that is no future now. Without Drago, I would not have been able to get this far."

"You give him too much credit," Daven told her. "You escaped him, so clearly, you have moved beyond what he can offer you."

"I think," came Lyle's deep voice, "that you should continue what you enjoy, but do so without the mercantile reasons that Drago Kramoris forced upon you."

Kina turned to look at Lyle behind her, and noted that Daven matched her sudden shift. Lyle sat on the ground with his back up against one of the packs, meticulously polishing his sword with a dark stained cloth. He seemed to take no notice of the attention he now had. Kina stared in surprise at him, stunned not by the advice that he had given, but by the fact that Lyle had spoken in such a way to her.

"That is a good idea," Daven spoke as he recovered from his own surprise first. He slapped Kina on the back with enough force that it forced the air from her lungs. "From what I've seen, you could easily rewrite much of the lost history of the Time of Gods and Magic."

"Not true," Kina said, rubbing her shoulder. "I don't know how to read."

Lyle looked to her, but Daven didn't look surprised. "But you said you remember everything."

"I do."

"Then you could learn to read and unlock the knowledge."

She again shook her head. If only it was that easy. Much of what she found was written in a language long forgotten. The figures were different from those written by the scholars of this time. Worse, finding somebody who would teach her would not be easy. She didn't have the backing of some royal noble or rich merchant. It was just her, with little to offer but her willingness to learn.

Lyle's laughter drew her out of her depression, and she looked back at him uncertainly.

"What's so funny?" Daven asked.

"You," Lyle answered, fixing Daven with a dark glare. "You spent days trying to teach the poor girl how to hold a blade, and yet what she most wants is to learn how to read. You could not be further from what interests her if you tried."

"That's not true!" Kina yelped, aghast by Lyle's observation.

Daven scratched the back of his head sheepishly. "I suppose a good sword battle is not exactly what a good girl dreams of," he responded with a chuckle of his own.

"But I want to be useful," Kina said, as much to hide her own discomfort on the subject as it was to prevent Daven from giving up on her.

Lyle slid his sword aside, and snorted loudly.

"Maybe I'm going about this the wrong way," Daven shrugged. "You move pretty quickly, perhaps I should focus on fighting skills."

"Daven," Lyle growled darkly, "only you could see the need to teach a young woman hand-to-hand combat."

"You're just jealous I found her first."

"Jealously is not an emotion I am feeling at this moment," Lyle said, though to Kina it almost sounded as though he were amused despite the gruff tone.

"Do puppets have emotions of their own?"

Lyle snorted again and looked away to the east. The back and forth barbs between the brothers had gone from playful to mean spirited in such a short period of time that it left Kina feeling confused and uncomfortable. For a moment, it had seemed Lyle was willing to open up.

"Why do you fight?" she asked, feeling the need to try some diplomacy.

"He started it!" Daven returned, pointing at his brother.

Lyle's response was one that gave her pause. He looked at her sadly and shook his head. "Sometimes old wounds do not heal." Daven made a disgusted noise and kicked at the ground.

"What did that mean?" she asked curiously. It was clear from Daven's face that she was not going to get an answer this night. Perhaps ever from Daven.

Lyle put his sword down on his pack and looked at Kina expectantly. "The topic, before my younger brother interrupted it, was you."

"But I don't know what I will do."

He frowned, but was not dissuaded. "Then tell me, Kina. Tell me about what you have learned about the source of that sword you carry."

"I really don't know much," Kina protested. She didn't want to open herself up to ridicule from Lyle, and his sudden interest in her was a little unsettling.

Daven didn't allow her to remain silent. "Such modesty. You know that it is named Vashnir, whatever that is, and that it once belonged to some goddess."

Lyle shifted his gaze to his brother before returning his attention to Kina. His look seemed to wander from surprise and curiosity to something that looked deeply troubled. "It belonged to a goddess?" The tone in his voice had become slightly strained and he looked agitated.

Kina stared at Daven. "You didn't tell him what we found in that ruin by the oasis?"

"Slipped my mind," Daven admitted, smiling at his brother nervously. Lyle rolled his eyes.

She sighed as she realized she had no choice but to explain.

"Nephrita. It belonged to Nephrita, daughter of Veran, the Goddess of Change. The sword is Vashnir."

Lyle regarded her sharply. "The Gods of Time are not spoken of in this day of age. Forgive my ignorance."

"Vast, vast ignorance," Daven added.

Lyle ignored him. "I know that they fell to the rightful Gods of Light, but beyond that I know very little."

Kina winced. She wondered if she could gracefully withdraw from this conversation. This was not a topic she wanted to openly discuss with somebody who believed in the preaching demanded by the Light. "What I tell you now," she said hesitantly, "is what I have learned through much travel. Do not simply dismiss what I say simply because it goes against what you have come to know.

"The Gods of Time did indeed claim these lands long ago. During their reign, magic prospered and powerful creatures of magic, such as malakhs and dragons, were more common. I hesitate to call them evil. Perhaps wrathful, but they did good in these lands too. They helped kingdoms of people to prosper in a dangerous world.

"The Gods of Light were said to arrive as much as a hundred lifetimes ago. They battled all that they deemed outside their own reign, bringing a war unlike any other in the history of our world. Nephrita, former owner of this sword, fought the strongest of the Gods of Light, Annasus. Neither returned to this world, though from the temple scriptures, Annasus was victor of this battle."

Kina looked over the land, seeing nothing larger than insects flying about the evening sky. "Magic began to fade. Those who could still call upon the power were persecuted by the temples of Light as being a follower of the fallen Gods of Time. Of the other races, they too have vanished over time. The ancient race which built the temple near Brighton disappeared sometime during this period. I believe the last dragon was seen during the lifetimes of the first Kings of Faneria."

Lyle took it in silence, and his expression suggested that he was listening to her. She was surprised that he allowed her to continue speaking what he may have seen as blasphemous lies.

"I know what a dragon is," Daven spoke up, smiling slyly at her. "There are enough legends of great battles against them. What is a malakh?"

Kina shrugged. "A creature of great power and magic. A servant of the gods. Something to that effect." Daven nodded, though she expected he had less an understanding of what that meant than she had. Malakhs were something of a mystery, spoken of rarely and often in connection to gods.

"Perhaps," Lyle stated, sounding somewhat uncertain, "perhaps it would be best if you did not put these stories into writing just yet. I would be careful of who it is you tell."

Kina nodded, but allowed herself a small smile. "I don't need to be told that."

"Indeed," Lyle shifted his legs where he sat and leaned his head back on the tree. "I believe you already know what you will do when you are freed of your curse, even if you do not yet realize it."

"What does that mean?" Kina asked.

Lyle refused to answer her, instead simply closing his eyes to the world. It appeared as though Lyle was through talking for now. She looked at Daven, who only shrugged and grinned at her.

Chapter Six

They lay on the ground, the three of them, watching the army that camped only a short distance away from the scant cover of the hill. Kina guessed there were as many as fifty men, and many had horses. They had built temporary fences to corral their horses, and erected tents to sleep within, but how long they had intended to stay was not a question Kina was capable of answering herself.

She listened instead to Daven and Lyle as they discussed the camp and the intentions of the men below based upon small observations she would have thought trivial. They were tense, and signs of worry creased Lyle's brow.

"They did not follow us," Lyle stated with certainty. "The fire pits show signs of previous use. They have camped here for several nights."

"Well, they couldn't have known we would come this way."

"Coincidence?"

"I hate coincidences. Fate hides surprises within coincidences."

"Oh be quiet."

"Look, they fly the Duke's colors, but they only have token sentries. They aren't here looking for us, but that doesn't mean they won't find us." Daven looked over to Kina, meeting her eyes for a brief moment. She felt a warmth inside her caused by the protective glance, and drew confidence from it. Daven smiled at her before looking at the camp again. He nodded, as if coming to some conclusion that he had yet to share.

"We can do this. The temple is just over that ridge. You can see the bell tower."

Kina looked harder and sure enough, past the camp, she could see the tall building peeking up over the next hill. She guessed it was no more than an hour's walk. It was, however, on the opposite side of the camp from where they lay now.

"It will take time," Lyle warned, "but if a mage calls the temples home I am willing to chance this."

"I have an idea," Daven said proudly. "Lyle, you take the horses and the packs and follow behind us."

Kina looked over at Daven, as did Lyle. Daven grinned widely as he looked down at the soldiers' camp, but did not expand on his idea. "That does not sound much like a plan to me."

"Lyle, all I want is for you to wait for us and keep an eye on the camp. Kina and I will go into the temple and talk to the mage. It'll be easier for us to get past the soldiers without the horses."

"Still not liking this," Lyle growled.

"It can work," Kina said at last. "I can be pretty sneaky."

"I am sure you can," snorted Lyle. "Why is it that I am not the one to see the mage?"

"Clearly, you must be the one to stay with the horses as you are the only one of us not already sought by the Duke," Daven answered, his voice sounding mocking, but Kina detected the faint strain revealing that even the roguish brother was tense.

She leaned closer to him and smiled warmly. "This will go fine. None shall see us." She slipped the hood off her ears and crawled backwards from the face of the hill. Getting past the camp was the least of her worries. Excitement and anticipation filled her soul leaving little room for thoughts of being captured. She was within reach of a magic user.

*   *   *

Kina gaped openly at the exterior walls of the monastery buildings. So much was hidden by the great walls surrounding the complex that she had hardly dreamed that it be as impressive. She knew the entire army camp lay on the other side of the walls, and yet there was no sign of them from where she stood. There were numerous small buildings with intricate patterns and decorations built into them. There was a bell hung only just above the ground, a bell so large that she could probably stand inside without being able to touch either side. There were people about as well, wearing brown, hooded robes that hid their faces from sight. She had come expecting dull and bleak and instead was treated to the exotic. She had no idea what it was these people worshiped, and she didn't recognize anything from the older religions.

Daven stopped beside her and whistled appreciatively. "Kind of makes you wonder."

"Wonder?" Kina asked, still awed.

"Wonder where they get the money for all this." He looked about and Kina noted there was no small amount of displeasure in what he saw. "You!" he cried at the nearest robed figure. "I need some answers."

Kina shot him a warning look and he merely shrugged in response. She stepped ahead of him, taking the lead away from him. As the person approached she wondered if her own cloak was as impressively deceptive. She had no idea what he looked like beneath the brown material.

"What is it you wish?" came a young voice from within. Very deceptive, Kina thought with a smile.

"We are here to find a great mage," she said firmly. "We have heard that one can be found here."

The figure remained silent for a moment, and Kina wondered if she had said something wrong. Perhaps magic was equally unwelcome here as it was through much of Edan? At last it seemed that the robed figure decided upon speaking.

"What mage? I know of none with that title within these walls." Kina felt disappointment well up inside her. She hadn't expected this.

"I see," Daven answered, his voice sounding odd to Kina's ears. "None, you say?"

"That is correct. Magic is not common in these lands."

"True, but not unheard of. What would you say if I told you that an enchanter lived here? One hiding from the Duke of Deverell?"

"I would say that you were mistaken."

"And that I intend to talk to this mage, even if it meant inviting the Duke's army, which is only just over that hill, into this place to find him."

Daven's threat caught both Kina and the young man off guard. She worried for a moment that he would do as he said, though belatedly realized that he would do no such thing. It was a bluff, or at least she hoped it was. The army that camped outside the walls was only a tool for Daven to intimidate the youth.

The young man sighed, and looked back at the largest of the temple buildings. "Why do you seek magic?"

"Knowledge," Kina stated firmly. "And perhaps help if I am favored."

The young man returned his attention upon Kina. "I am not stupid, I do not believe you are allied with the Duke. Who are you?"

"Daven Hitchcliffe," Daven offered, pushing Kina aside. She did not remain silent, despite Daven's attempt to hide the truth.

"My name is Kina Ukiel," she offered. There was recognition of the name, a sure sign that news from Brighton had already arrived. Fortunately, it appeared that the young man had little intention of turning her in to the Duke.

"The Mad Duke is not welcome within these walls," the young

man told her, his tone not unfriendly. "However, I do not understand your wish to see the one within."

Daven stepped close to Kina and she could feel his protective aura encircle her. "I would think that any good mage of any power would willingly help those in need."

"You assume that she is good."

"Is she not?" Kina asked.

"She has killed many in these lands. Have you not heard of the Dark Witch of Tanara?"

Kina heard Daven curse. She looked at him questioningly while she answered, "I have not."

Daven supplied the details for her. "The Dark Witch is otherwise named Nadia of Tanara, a construct created with the darkest of enchantments. She became one of the most evil warlords to walk this land. She even managed to carve herself a bit of Edan which she was able to call her own."

The young man was not content to leave the story incomplete. "When she rode her army down from the spires of the Dragon's Teeth eight years ago, it took ten thousand men under command of the king himself to finally defeat her within the shadow of this very place."

Kina stood aghast. Her hopes of finding a cure here had been dashed in moments before she had even spoken to the enchantress. "But why keep her here if she was so evil? Why not at one of the castles, or executed for her crimes?"

Daven had no answer, but the young man apparently knew of one. "It is said that the king spoke with Nadia at great length following her eventual defeat. She was brought here under armed guard and imprisoned within these walls. Orders direct from the king strictly stated that she remain here, for the remainder of her life. More, that the Duke, Lord Gawthrain, would not be permitted entrance."

That was interesting, Kina thought. The obvious connection

was that the king had not wanted the enchantress to fall into the hands of the Duke.

"Of course, the king died mere months following the end of the conflict," Daven noted. "That put you in a bit of a bind because now you were stuck with a criminal within your walls."

"That is not for me to say," the young man answered with a shrug. "Nor is it my say whether or not you may see the abomination, if that is still your wish."

Daven's eyes fell on Kina, and she considered her decision carefully. If Nadia was indeed an expert on enchantments, then she would be able to provide support that few others could. If she were willing. She met Daven's eyes and nodded gently. She wanted to take the chance anyway.

Daven sighed and looked to the younger man. "Apparently, we do."

"Very well," the young man answered, sounding pained. "I will take you to the Elder."

They were led through the interior of one of the smaller buildings by the young man, who had yet to give his own name. Kina considered that mystery only briefly, before deciding it was unimportant. With any luck they would speak with this Nadia of Tanara and be gone shortly. She had little intention of ever returning to this place once she had spoken to the enchantress.

The interior of the building, despite the outside appearance, was startlingly barren. The walls had no decorations, no columns or any other kind of fancy architecture that she would have expected from such buildings. She could see some truth in that they lived here without need of such extravagance. When she considered the interior, she realized even the exterior was only stunning by the size and style of construction. It wasn't rich, it was merely different from what she was used to.

The young man knocked once on an open door before them,

before turning and waving them forward to enter. Inside, an elderly man sat behind a big table, his hood down so that all could see his face. The scrolls littering the room drew Kina's curious eyes, but her emotions were easily stilled. Knowledge, it seemed, was something these people hoarded.

"Master," the young man said with a slight bow to the elder, "these people have come to speak with the witch."

That seemed to put life in the old figure. He sat up straighter, and his eyes opened wider as his focus was drawn up from the table. "Indeed?" There was humor in his voice, but Kina noted the way Daven tensed at the single spoken word. "I am Yusef, senior priest of these grounds. Please, introduce yourselves." He looked Kina's way and she noted the suspicion within his eyes. She wondered if it was caused by their request, or the fact that she hid herself beneath the cloak much like their own members. "Tell me why I should trust you to visit with our secret guest."

"Daven Hitchcliffe," Daven stated formally, dipping his head respectfully. "From Faneria."

"I have heard of you," the priest snorted, his voice sounding disrespectful. "Destroyed a castle on the border, if I recall correctly. Quite the achievement for a bandit. I do not see why I should allow you to stay within these walls any longer than it would take to escort you from them." Yusef turned his ancient eyes to Kina's hooded form next.

"Kina Ukiel," she said softly.

"Kina Ukiel the thief? Kina Ukiel the assassin?" The old man scowled. "Do not hide yourself in my presence when you come asking for favors."

Daven shifted and looked to her warningly, and Kina hesitated a moment knowing she shouldn't, but what choice did she have? She removed the hood of her cloak, and stood calmly amidst the tense air. The old man sputtered and coughed loudly while the younger unnamed man fell back against the door and stared at her with fear. Daven put his hand upon his sword, wary of any sign of attack. Kina simply stood still and watchful.

The old man took a moment to regain his breath and coughed twice more as he tried to speak again. "I would be lying if I had said that your name is unknown here," he said with a strained sounding voice. "What the Duke's messenger failed to note was that you were a construct."

"I am not a construct," Kina replied firmly. "I was human not long ago. I was transformed into this monster before the Duke's very eyes."

"And escaped from the heart of his domain," Yusef coughed again. "Interesting." He shifted in his seat and closed his eyes thoughtfully. "You wanted to see the witch, you say?"

"I hope that she would know of a cure to my curse."

"Unlikely, at best. And what would you do if you were cured?"

Kina opened her mouth before realizing that she didn't have an answer to give. She hesitated, giving thought to her answer. Lyle had suggested she continue her trade, and in truth she knew of nothing else she would enjoy more. Specifically, she knew of one mystery she needed to solve. "I would continue my quest to unlock the mysteries of the Blade of Vashnir."

The old man's eyes lit up brilliantly and he rose to his feet, surprised and intrigued by what she said. "The blade carried by the patron of Chaos? Whatever for?"

Daven's hand touched her own, both warning her of giving too much away, and providing warm support. She clasped his hand and gave a firm squeeze of her own. "The Duke Gawthrain hired me to retrieve it. I would much rather know why he would want for it, and what dangers this would present."

"The Duke seeks a sword from legend?" Yusef sat down again and looked out his sole window. He looked older, frail, as he sat motionless. She hoped her honesty had convinced him that she needed to see Nadia for a cure. At the very least, perhaps she had appealed to his sense of compassion. She fought the urge to fidget, and tightened her grip on Daven's hand.

Eventually, Yusef swung his chair forward to face her once more. He smiled peacefully, giving her hope that he would see her reasoning. "Balcome!" he barked loudly, and she started at both the volume and forcefulness of it.

"Yes Master!" The young man fairly jumped in fright as he refocused himself upon his elder.

"I will not allow any visitors. The witch was entrusted to us by the king, and we shall not fail him." Kina opened her mouth to protest, but she noted the sly look on the old man's face. "However, somebody capable of evading the Duke is likely to slip through our defenses. Please, see to it that they find the door."

"Master?" Balcome seemed confused, but she and Daven understood his meaning.

"Thank you," she responded, bowing slightly.

"I hope you find what you are looking for," Yusef said gravely, "but I would not expect to find help here. The witch is not a hospitable person."

Kina nodded respectfully. As she followed the others out of the room, she saw a glimpse of concern on the elderly man. It was gone in an instant, but Kina pondered the momentary break in the man's expression. She had certainly delivered plenty of potential trouble in an already unstable land.

She followed Balcome deeper into the building, going down more stairs than there were floors above ground. Without windows, the light was provided only by the torch he carried. He stopped outside a door and turned to face them, hesitating a moment as if unsure of what to say. At long last he sighed and stepped back to allow her to pass.

"If you are certain of your choice, you may enter. I will wait for you here."

She nodded, and gave Daven a glance over her shoulder to

confirm that he was still with her. The look on his face suggested that he would follow her to the ends of the world, and that they may in fact be fast approaching it. She grinned in response to his expression, grateful to have him with her.

Opening the door she was greeted by more stairs, fading into the darkness. Nothing but black beyond.

"Do I need a torch?" she asked Balcome with some confusion.

"No light is permitted to enter. We still do not know the extent of her powers. She is truly the first artificial malakh known to us. It would be safer that she does not see."

"But if we cannot see," Kina said, looking at the wooden stairs unhappily, "we could fall."

"It is the rules," Balcome responded firmly.

"How do you feed her?" Daven asked, sounding annoyed with the younger man. "Obviously somebody must go down there."

Balcome smiled faintly, looking somewhat sympathetic. "There are fifty-seven stairs and five landings. We follow the wall with one hand on it at all times."

Kina shivered at the thought of traveling in complete darkness. She squinted down the stairs and wondered how well her vision would be to this new challenge. She took a couple of steps forward past the entrance way. Daven moved to follow but she raised her hand to wave him back.

"Please. Close the door for a moment."

Daven hesitated but took a step back. She had no doubt he was confused, but she didn't want to look back into the light. She needed her eyes to adjust to the darkness. The door slowly closed behind her and her world became darkness. She stared hard at where she knew the stairs had been. Nothing. She drew the hood back from her head and continued to wait patiently for her eyes to adjust. It took time, but she began to make out the edges of objects. The ledge of each stair began to appear faintly in the darkness, as did the rough stone wall. She could see in the dark.

Another side to her curse that she had so far been unaware of. Little wonder that she had so little trouble seeing at night.

She turned and tried to open the door only to find that it lacked a latch to do so. If this witch got this far from her prison, she wondered whether a door without latch would give her any pause. Kina knocked twice and waited for the door to flood light back into her life. She closed her eyes at the sharp painful light that greeted her, but she had learned what she needed.

Kina looked back to Daven and shrugged. "I will be fine, but you will be unable to see anything. Would you rather stay here?"

"Just be sure not to let me trip," Daven remarked unhappily. So he was coming with her. It was comforting to know that she had friends. She started walking down without further pause, taking each stair carefully. She hoped Daven would be able to see her if he stayed close. Several stairs down she felt his hand on her shoulder.

"Just lead," he said simply. "I will follow."

The stairs led downward through several flights. Each ended at a small landing before turning to the right and beginning with a new flight. It was a slow climb down with Daven blind. She herself had troubles seeing in total darkness. The fact that she could at all was a surprise that she felt little comfort in. She stepped down softly, feeling each step before putting any weight on it. It was slow, but she would rather see that they both arrived safely.

"Only a few more stairs," Kina told him.

"What is that awful smell?" Daven asked with annoyance. Kina shrugged, belatedly realizing that he would have to feel the motion rather than see it.

"They do not clean my cage often," another woman spoke, a cruel edge to her voice despite sounding amused. "After a few months, you grow used to it."

"Nadia?" Kina asked hopefully.

"Well, I'm the only one down here," the woman answered. Kina looked about, seeing very little of help in the small room. It wasn't very large, but it was larger than the room she stayed at the inn in Brighton. There was another locked door, with a tiny barred window into the cell. It was too high to see through however, so she couldn't see any shapes within. "You speak as if you have searched for me. One wonders how you have come to find me in this place."

"A blind man," Daven remarked dryly. "Apparently he can see what cannot be seen."

"A blind man," Nadia repeated thoughtfully. Kina could almost hear the sly smile in the tone of her voice. "You were sent to see my dark hole by a vision provided by blindness. Why?"

"We have come to ask your help," Daven said carefully.

"My help?" She laughed loudly, a sound of pleasure tainted with hate. "People have sought me for many things in my life," she said darkly. "Help has never been one of them."

"Please," Kina responded. "I have been cursed, and I need your help."

"Curses are funny things," Nadia responded from the darkness. "They have a certain smell to them, and the magic that feeds them glows within my mind. I see no curse upon you. The only curse in this prison is my own. No, I cannot help you."

Kina bit her lip as her eyes lowered to the floor. Hope, it seemed, was too much to ask for.

Daven, however, seemed unsatisfied by the answer. "Are you not powerful enough to help?"

There was a challenge laid, and it drew out life from the enchantress. Kina could feel the dark arrogance the woman wrapped herself with. "Oh, I am plenty powerful. There are few that could ever claim to have the power that I am able to call upon. I tell no lie when I say there is no curse on your woman, there. Magic, yes, wild and uncontrolled, but it is not her. An object she carries is bound with the magic. Very powerful." There was a pause, but the voice that continued seemed genuinely curious and interested, and lacked the edge. "I have seen many enchanted items, but this is above and beyond any work of man. What is it that you bring to me?"

Kina hesitated before speaking. She listened to the air, noting a familiar sound that she knew would lead to trouble. That was the sound of armored men marching down wooden stairs, and that sound was becoming louder. Trouble.

"Well, would you tell me?" Nadia's voice floated through the darkness. "It will do you no harm to sate my curiosity, would it?"

"Daven," Kina whispered harshly, her hand falling to Vashnir at her side. "We need to go."

"Yet you have not received the help you have come for," Nadia noted teasingly. "Tell me about the object. Did the blind man know?"

"What is it?" Daven asked, ignoring the enchantress.

"Soldiers," she whispered, pulling her hood up over her head.

"There have been none of those in years," Nadia growled firmly. Kina didn't have time to argue otherwise as she realized that it was too late. A dozen armed soldiers had come through the door upstairs, and they had no hesitation in bringing down torches. Kina shielded her eyes against the onslaught of light.

"More visitors?" Nadia snapped at the men sharply. "It seems I've become important once more."

"Quiet, wench," hissed the one in the lead. "We have come to return you to Brighton."

Daven drew his sword, and pushed Kina behind him. It was a hopeless battle, but Kina could see no alternative. It took a moment to register that the soldier had said he had come for Nadia, and not for them. Even though his sword was drawn, Daven was attracting only the minimum of attention.

"I see." Nadia spoke with warning. "Know this, if you attempt to force me to leave these grounds, I will stand against you. Be gone." There was a sound of metal sliding against leather, and Kina looked back at the locked door uncertainly. The confidence with which Nadia spoke made it sound as though she was no prisoner.

"If these two interfere, take them as well," the leader ordered, stepping aside to let his men down the stairs. Daven tensed, but Kina held him back from advancing. He lowered his sword, but held it tightly within his hand.

"Something isn't right here," Daven whispered for her ears only. "I don't like that they have orders to bring her to Brighton." She could hardly argue. Hadn't the old man told them that she was an enemy of the Duke?

The sound of a strange language being whispered filtered through the darkness, followed by the sound of wood cracking. Kina flinched and looked back at the wooden door, which looked fairly solid, but was quickly developing large cracks accompanied by violent snapping sounds. The soldiers too noticed the sounds and uncertainty stayed their feet. All at once the door blew out and shards of wood flew outward. Kina threw herself at the floor, avoiding the missiles that flew straight through where she and Daven stood. Daven lay on the other side of the doorway looking bewildered and frightened. The soldiers that had come down the stairs had not been so lucky. A torch fell to the ground, and several men tumbled down to the dirt packed floor. Others drew swords and hurried down, but were slowed by their fallen comrades.

Through this, Kina's eyes returned to the prison cell. A woman, smaller than she, stepped through the now open doorway into the torch lit chamber. Despite the added light from the torches, Nadia still appeared to be wrapped within shadow. Only her shape could be distinguished through them.

"Draw your sword, girl." Nadia growled at her. "Get out of the dirt and fight." The enchantress opened her right hand revealing one of the bars from her door. She gripped it tightly and began walking forward. Kina watched as the soldiers slowed and halted their advance. Daven backed out of the way and let the small woman step by. Despite her size, it was clear she had a presence that none wanted to test.

"What's the matter?" she asked, the cruel edge back in her voice. "I thought you cared not for what I wished. I stand before you now. Me, a mere woman, and I ask you if you are brave enough to face me in battle." Kina slid back away, putting her back to the cold stone wall. What had she released into this world? Even as she watched Nadia stand within the torch light, she could tell the enchantress was gaining in strength. The shadows that circled her grew darker and multiplied. They became more defined, becoming shapes, figures and unfamiliar characters. This was no mere mage, Kina realized. An artificial malakh, the priest Yusef had said, a demi-goddess in her own right.

Nadia raised the bar before her as though it were a weapon, challenging the soldiers. Their expressions made it clear that they did not want to test the enchantress in the darkness of the underground prison. "Now run along," she ordered the soldiers. "I have things to do, and I'm most certain you do not want to die here."

Kina watched as those that were able to scrambled up the stairs as fast as they could. Those that were wounded moved at a pace that belied their injuries. Nadia ignored the last of them, turning her attention on Kina. "I believe I told you to get up," she said with impatience.

"Hold it," Daven snapped, sliding in behind Nadia gracefully, and sliding his sword up against the side of the woman's throat. Kina hadn't realized he had moved from her side within the shadows. He seemed to tower over Nadia, the size difference was so great. "Magic is such a pain," he remarked with a surprisingly light tone.

"You do realize they won't go far, right?" Nadia remained still, though her eyes met Kina's own. "Surely you want my help."

"We can do well without it," Daven answered firmly. "I fear the cost of your help would be too great."

"I offer my help freely," she returned, smirking slightly. "I'm no longer safe here."

"Safe?" Kina repeated. "With your power who could stop you?"

Nadia smirked proudly. "Few. There are those, however, that could hold power over me still. I agreed to hide here in penance for my crimes, but it would appear that it was all for naught."

Daven looked shaken from behind the strange woman. "Wait, you agreed to hide here?"

"Look, are you going to move that sword?" Annoyance flashed over her face, before she blew out a breath in exasperation. "Yes. Yes, I agreed to be imprisoned here. I'm a monster," her eyes locked onto Kina's again and she flashed a grin. "You have the gift of mage sight, you can see me for what I am," she told her, pretty much ignoring Daven and the sword he held at her neck. "Tell him, what do you see when you look at me?"

Kina hesitated. "I see dark circles of strange characters floating around her, dozens of them. More characters cover her skin. And they move." Kina shivered.

"Enchantments," Nadia added. "I have layers of magic upon my body. Spells cast upon me while I was young still. I am not of your kind." The small woman's face shifted as she studied Kina. "Whatever your kind is."

"What kind of spells?"

"That is my business, not yours," Nadia remarked, as though she seemed uninterested in the current topic of discussion. "Even if you were to cut my throat, I would not die," she told Daven pointedly.

Daven hesitated and then withdrew the sword from Nadia's neck, though the woman didn't react to the change. Instead she shared a look with Kina, one that Kina understood well. Nadia had not wanted the life she was forced to live, nor did she much like it herself.

"You want to be normal," Kina said for all to hear.

The woman laughed darkly. "Not quite," she returned. "What I want is not possible in any event. The enchantments are part of me. To remove them would be my death. You on the other hand look like somebody who wants to become a human. I would guess the extra features are what you thought a curse, hmm?"

"How can it not be a curse?"

"It was magic, certainly, but not a curse that made you this way." Nadia looked back to the stairway and threw the metal bar on the ground. It clattered loudly, as it found fragments of metal in the dirt. "They are waiting for us at the next landing."

"So what you are saying is, if we help you escape, you will help us?" Daven slid his sword away, but watched the enchanted woman warily.

"I have no need for your help," Nadia laughed. "You need mine."

"Not true," Kina said as she sat up. "You need us."

"What?" Anger flashed over the small woman's face. "I could escape from here at any time. I chose to do so now because I want to."

"True," Kina replied. She stood and drew Vashnir from her side. "You are powerful beyond what we can ever know. What has that power done for you in your life, I wonder? Why has Lord Gawthrain sent men to collect you?"

Nadia sneered back at Kina. "Gawthrain is a fool," she growled. "What he plans does not concern me." There was doubt here, however, and Kina could see the momentary flash in her eyes as it betrayed her. It seemed the great and powerful Nadia had her own fears of the Duke.

"You know." Daven hazarded a guess in slow and cautious tones. "You know what he plans."

Again the woman looked uncomfortable, and she glared at Daven for a moment. "Perhaps," she returned. "And I see no reason why I should tell you anything."

"The Duke looks for an enchantress," Kina noted, and she raised Vashnir so that she could support its weight with both hands. She cupped the blade with her left so that Nadia could see the shape of the weapon, if not the details. She questioned how clearly even Nadia could see within the poor light of the fallen torches. "The Duke also comes for the sword."

"The sword," Nadia repeated, suddenly enthralled by the sight of it. Kina stepped back uncertainly as the woman took a determined stride forward. Was it something that about the sword that called to the witch, or was it knowledge of the weapon itself that drew the reaction?

"No," Kina said, holding the weapon away. "For the time being this is mine."

"That is the object which changed you," Nadia declared. "Its magic gives it away. Give it to me so it can do no further damage."

Kina made a show of putting it away within its scabbard at her side. "No. First, tell me what you know of Vashnir."

Whatever Nadia thought she knew of the sword, it became well apparent that she had been mistaken. Upon hearing the name she recoiled away and her eyes flashed from sword to Kina's eyes in an instant. "You lie," she hissed, though her voice was little more than a whisper.

"The ghosts we encountered," Daven argued, "were most convincing."

"The dead have their own agenda," Nadia dismissed.

"However, if it is the weapon known as Vashnir, it would be a bad omen."

"Why would it be a bad omen?"

"Fools," Nadia snapped impatiently. "It is one of the few items of power to be created by the gods, a fact alone that should make any mortal wary of claiming ownership of it." Nadia shrugged dismissively. "Assuming of course that you now hold onto the true Vashnir, I would not rate your odds of survival as high."

"Nephrita was defeated by Annasus," Kina argued. "She is not coming back."

"Perhaps." Nadia looked distant for a moment. "And what if Veran or her blood were to come to you and request that you release her? Would you do it?" Nadia glanced at Daven. "What if Annasus returns and decides that your possession of the sword is a sign that you intend to release her? Who knows what any of the others may think? One does not involve themselves with the likes of gods."

While Nadia's thoughts were concerning, these too were not new to Kina. She had already considered the implications of holding onto Nephrita's sword, and dismissed them. "The sword is not yours to be concerned over."

"And for that I am thankful. I am already involved with gods too much already." Nadia looked as though she was reconsidering something. The small woman did speak her mind after only a moment of thought. "Gawthrain wants for the sword, you say?"

"That is the truth," Kina answered.

"I may have prematurely dismissed how dangerous that would be."

Daven, ever watchful of the stairwell, glanced through the shadows at Nadia. "Why's that?"

"Tell me, do you know who advises Gawthrain within his court?"

"Not off hand, no," Daven answered. Kina could only shake

her head.

"And you say that a blind man sent you here to see me?"

Kina hesitated at the strange questions. "Yes," she answered tightly.

Nadia looked first into her cell and then to the stairs. "Very well. First we escape this place. If you still wish to part ways, we can do so at that point. I do intend to stir up trouble in this region, so if you don't want direct confrontation with the Duke, then perhaps it's wise we part ways." She snorted loudly. "I do expect to see the sword again in my future, whether it be in your hand or another owner. Gawthrain will not rest until it is his. How the likes of you managed to come this far with it in your possession escapes me."

"The Duke has to find us before he can take it from us."

"Truth. If you can evade the Duke in his own land, perhaps you are stronger than you appear." Nadia looked up the stairs again. "They are getting restless," she noted. She grinned at Kina darkly. "Wait here three minutes and then walk up the stairs after me. Do not run, but do not hesitate. The way will be clear."

She started forward and Daven paused a moment before stepping clumsily forward. He held his sword up to the witch, who already stood several stairs up. "Take this, it would do me no good anyway. My eyes will need to adjust to the light."

Nadia nodded once. "I shall return it to you when we reach the ground level." She accepted the sword and continued marching upward slowly. Kina held her breath and watched the woman go. It seemed wrong to let her go, but at the same time frightening the way she had suddenly decided to take things upon herself. She looked to Daven but he was concerning himself more with collecting a torch and a discarded sword from the dirt floor.

"Are we just going to let her go?"

"In tight quarters, we would be in the way. She has a better chance on her own than if I was trying to fight by her side.

Secondly, it's known that the witch was a ferocious fighter. Those soldiers were not afraid because of her kicking out the door. They have heard the same tales I have."

"But, there are so many of them!"

"Only so many can fight her at a time within a stairwell." Daven looked up the stairs, and with the help of the torch she was able to make out his unhappy expression. "I'm not sure that I want the witch to survive."

"She knows something," Kina pointed out. "Something we don't."

"But if the witch survives, it would complicate matters."

And that, Kina wondered thoughtfully, might be true. She could not help but wonder what knowledge could be gained by speaking with Nadia further. She smiled darkly to herself as she thought of her companions. It seemed she drew the lowlifes of the world to her. Mercenaries, thieves and warlords. Perhaps it was the company most suited for a monster, but she was beginning to wonder if perhaps she was fated for something grand. The gods might have reason for providing powerful friends for her. She gripped the handle of Vashnir at her side, reminding herself that there was purpose. Change was stirring in these lands.

While the trip back to land lit by daylight offered no perils, it was a journey that Kina found very discomforting. She was grateful that it was relatively brief and poorly lit. It appeared that an army had journeyed this path and waged a bloody battle. It would also appear Nadia took no prisoners as she advanced, and that even soldiers sent by the lord of this land were no match for the witch.

Kina did not see the body of Balcome among the dead, but the faces of the soldiers were now locked within her memories. She had never seen so many dead in a single place before. Having a perfect memory was not always a gift.

Daven spoke little as she led him swiftly past the fallen. Once freed from the darkness he took the lead. The hallways were silent now. Kina doubted that Nadia had ventured far from her path. The blood suggested that she had been very focused upon cutting an exit through the massed army. Kina took hope in that. The lives that normally rested within these walls were laying silent. Fearful of the terror that had been released from within. It would seem that she was destined for further complications.

Daven looked at her briefly before flashing an unreadable smile. With a nod he swung around and out the door back into the light of the sun outside. His feet shuffled to a stop there, however. In confusion, Kina followed him around. Outside was not a great army awaiting them. It was strangely silent, absent of those who had strolled so casually through the grounds that morning. Instead stood Nadia, a small, pale woman dressed in dark leathers and covered in blood and dirt. In her hands she held Daven's sword, and Lyle's hair as she held him in at her mercy. Strangely, the look on Lyle's face was one of disappointment rather than fear.

"I see your taste in women is improving," he said flatly.

"What are you doing here?" Daven asked. Nadia released Lyle unceremoniously and looked skyward, a strange expression on her face that left Kina wondering what it meant.

"I was trying to rescue you," Lyle growled. "Gods know why I should care. Who is this one?"

"Best you not ask," Daven answered.

Kina looked at the smaller woman. This was the mighty warlord, the witch that was so feared? Kina wondered if she had seemed so insignificant prior to the curse. Nadia did seem to carry herself with confidence, however, and Kina could not avoid the feelings of discomfort she felt just being near her. The only object on her that seemed more for appearance than function was an ornate looking pendant that hung around her neck on a simple chain.

Nadia took notice of her stare belatedly. Her expression

hardened, and the warrior returned.

"I see," she said simply as her eyes traveled over Kina. Kina was baffled to what that meant.

"Nadia, I do want my sword back at some point," Daven said, taking notice in the witch's sudden interest in Kina. The small woman shifted, and tossed the blade without interest in Daven's direction. It dropped into the earth blade first near his feet, seemingly controlled without a hand to guide it. Daven glanced at her and tossed away the sword he had collected from the prison.

"Nadia?" Lyle repeated, his voice already sounding as though he was not going to like what he heard next.

Nadia's attention finally drawn from Kina, the witch smiled darkly at Lyle and bowed deeply to him. "The blight of Tanara, that's me." She grinned, an odd lopsided look, and put her hand on her hip expectantly. "My reputation is still with power, I see."

Lyle looked on, and then turned back to Daven without change in his expression. "I was wrong. You are beyond salvation."

"Great," Daven remarked. "Thanks. Okay, new plan. I think we should put some space between us and this temple. I doubt we'll have many friends in the region when word gets out about this."

"The legend of Daven Hitchcliffe grows another head," Lyle growled, slowly getting to his feet. It would seem to Kina that all agreed to Daven's suggestion of retreating.

"Where are the horses?" Daven asked, looking about warily.

"On the far side of the temple complex." Lyle began to run at a brisk pace Kina found easy to match. The four of them looked about, alert for trouble, but it would seem that there were no surprises lying in wait for them. "I saw the soldiers move in, and the residents flee. No surprise as to why that might be." Lyle glanced at Nadia. "Did we find what we were looking for?"

"Not exactly," Daven answered.

Nadia wasn't to be baited into an argument, however. She simply ran along silently, a sword in her hands that Kina guessed she had taken up from one of the many that had been dropped to the ground. Lyle too remained silent. She hoped he wasn't too angry with her for freeing the witch.

They made their escape with ease, disappearing into the distance before nightfall. Much of the hastened journey was done in silence. Kina wondered what occupied their thoughts. Were they simply focused upon their escape or as unnerved by the witch as she was?

They made camp in the failing sunlight, an unknown distance from the temples. Kina turned her attention to the path they had traveled, listening for danger, but it seemed they were not pursued.

Nadia stepped away from the group, watching the horizon to the north. The dark emblems encircling her seemed all the more frightening in daylight, and Kina fought the urge to shudder away. Nadia's eyes sought and found Kina's own. "I would like to accompany you," she said with conviction. She glanced to Daven and Lyle and nodded in their direction as well. "If you would have me, I would swear my service to your quest."

"Why?" Daven asked, the tone of his voice suggesting that he didn't like Nadia's offer. Kina turned, and noted that even Lyle had taken interest in Daven's attitude.

"Why what?" Nadia asked.

"Why would you offer your abilities to us? Why should we accept that offer?"

"The second is easy," Nadia returned. "I offer you strength that you would not be able to match in these lands. I am not afraid of the Duke, and I willingly take up arms against him. You need allies, and I would be a powerful one. I have other reasons that I will not tell you, but suffice to say I have powerful friends.

"The first is a bit harder to explain." Nadia shifted and looked north once more. "For that, I must ask you, what have you heard of me?"

Kina shrugged. She could not answer this. Daven, however, showed no hesitation. He spat on the ground and glared at the witch. "You and your dark army stormed into the southern provinces of Edan, taking Tanara and the surrounding towns under your control. From there, you tortured the townsfolk and waged war upon the rightful king of Edan."

Nadia smirked, looking more amused than angered. "I said: what have you heard of me? Not my exploits in recent wars and political affairs. And as a note, there is little truth in what you have said. I'm impressed by your rage however. Did I not do Faneria a favor in distracting Edan's attention inward?"

Kina sensed the bait, and interrupted before Daven could answer. "Tell us of yourself. I for one have not heard of you during my travels."

"Indeed?" Nadia refocused her gaze upon Kina, a sly look on her face suggesting she must have recognized the subtle diffusing tactics. "How about you?" she asked Lyle. "Have you heard of my origins?"

Lyle's expression seemed to shift from discontentment to confusion. "No. The stories I heard all begin with you riding into Tanara one morning with your army."

Nadia nodded in acceptance of Lyle's honesty. She returned to Daven once again. "And you?"

Kina could see that despite his hatred, he had an answer to the question. "I heard you were created by dark mages in a ritual meant to create an unstoppable soldier."

Nadia didn't flinch at his words. She gazed at him for a period of time that stretched long beyond what Kina felt was comfortable. At last, Nadia nodded, smiling faintly. "Fool," she muttered. Her amusement melted away as she looked to the sky and then to the north. "I was indeed born to this world, not created like some construct. I won't get into too much detail, but my upbringing had little to do with who I am now. You miss on some crucial facts and draw more upon normal paranoid rumors and gossip."

Nadia crossed her arms under her chest and looked strangely calm. "I am very old." She didn't look all that old, Kina thought with confusion. "I outlived the small kingdom my father once ruled over. My people are memories only."

"Wyecroft," Kina guessed, drawing the name from an old tome she had discovered along the coast of Faneria. An old man read it to her aloud, sometimes sounding amazed and others disbelieving. She could recall the look on his face as he turned each page, the expressions often telling that there were more to the pages than he read to her.

It would seem that she was correct, as Nadia showed signs of surprise, and perhaps even a moment of happiness. "And how is it you have heard of that?"

"Wyecroft once ruled the mountains and the foothills. Tanara would have fallen within its borders during the Time of Gods and Magic."

Daven snorted, clearly unimpressed. "So that was your justification for sacking the town?" Lyle socked him over the head with a closed fist, silencing the younger brother. Daven rubbed his head while glaring at his brother but Lyle wasn't paying him any attention.

"If you are as old as that tale," Lyle grumbled loudly, "then you would be more than two hundred cycles of age."

"So I would," she returned. "Older still in fact." Kina felt a spring of joy and wonder fill within her. The revelation must have been obvious, for Nadia shook her head at her. "I may be old, but wise I am not. I have not lived a joyous life, nor one of the scholar. I am only a warrior. The gods are not kind to lesser beings, no matter what the stories tell. Not the Gods of Light, not the gods of old."

"Why Tanara?" Lyle asked, sounding doubtful, but curious.

"Have you not journeyed there? Asked the people of Tanara of their just and noble rulers? Asked the questions of where a fabled demoness drew the many for her armies?" A wicked smile crossed her lips, one which was cruel and angry. "Overburdened by the taxes of unseen royalty, Tanara overthrew the soldiers of Edan. I came with only a dozen men, sent by the king himself to put down the rebellion. We were mercenaries, but when we arrived we did not draw our swords against the farmers and merchants. The foothills of the Dragon's Teeth are formidable in their own ways. A few could hold against the many. A hundred could stand against an army. A thousand could defeat a kingdom. When Edan's armies came, our archers rained down death upon them from the mountain passes."

A chill passed through Kina's body as she understood why Edan had feared Nadia. She had joined the peasant revolt and had shown them how to defend themselves. She found comfort in the thought, and was strangely pleased by the imagery of mighty nobles being thwarted by peasants.

"By the light of the gods," Lyle whispered, apparently likewise impressed.

An odd smirk now crossed Daven's lips. "You resurrected your kingdom?"

Nadia laughed haughtily, again disagreeing with the rogue. "Hardly. We built no walls. We had no castle. The taxes were reduced to a pittance. The core of the army was small, and required little upkeep. Witch of Tanara I may be to the kingdom of Edan, but to the town of Tanara I was a celebrated hero."

"So you expect us to believe that you should be thanked for your selfless acts of generosity?" Daven asked with a sneer.

"No, I expect that you realize that not all said of me is truth."

Lyle put his hand on his brother's shoulder, his firm grip calming his sibling as the larger man stepped up to his full height.

"If what you say is true, how is it you come to be in a prison here?"

"The full wrath of Edan fell upon us, and the King himself rode into battle with a force ten thousand strong. I took my army and fled from the village into the plains to meet our enemy in order to protect the town. The king promised my people would be spared if I surrendered to him. The figurehead removed, the precious image of invulnerability defeated, Tanara was forced to rejoin the kingdom.

"King Morgan was a just ruler, and a good man. Flawed certainly, he had no small amount of arrogance and his ambition was unmatched, but he had not brought the people to the point of rebellion in Tanara. For that, one need only look to another ambitious noble seeking to raise his own army in secret."

Nadia fixed Daven with a look of fierce hatred. "Gawthrain."

"Revenge? Is that what you want?" Kina asked.

"It is among the reasons I wish to see him dead. I don't like the thought of Edan falling into his hands."

"I would accept your help," Kina told the enchanted warrior. She looked to Lyle and Daven for support in her decision and found herself disappointed by the reactions of the pair. Lyle simply shrugged indifferently, while Daven threw his hands up in defeat and walked away.

"A sentiment not shared by your companions it would seem," Nadia remarked with faint smile.

"Daven is stubborn," Lyle remarked flatly. "It will take much to sway him."

"I respect his honest emotions," Nadia nodded to Lyle. "I am no angel and I do deserve much of his hatred, though perhaps not for the reasons he believes. How about you? Clearly you have your own opinions."

"I have not yet decided," Lyle answered gruffly. "I have none but your word against the many who trade in rumors. As you say, you deserve such emotions and this does not make it easy to accept you. I do not like you, but for now I see wisdom in joining forces. This may change if you become more hindrance than help."

A dark laugh emanated from Nadia and she spread her arms wide. "I do not ask for your compassion. You can hate me if it eases the burdens on your soul."

"I do not hate for my own sake," Lyle responded, a strangeness in his voice that Kina found interesting. "I agree to work with you for that is what has been decided. Your actions will decide how I treat you. I wonder, though, why is it that you wish for people to hate you?"

Nadia grimaced, and her posture shifted ever so slightly. "None of your concern," she returned in a tone that suggested it was not something she enjoyed thinking about.

Lyle touched her shoulder gently. "That was a question that need not be answered for my ears." Lyle walked off, refusing to allow the conversation to go further despite a suddenly protesting Nadia. The woman looked to Kina, her face questioning and strangely uncertain. Kina shrugged, wondering who of the two of them was more surprised by Lyle's actions.

With one last sigh, Nadia straightened herself to her full height and her expression stiffened. "Perhaps you can explain to me why you look as you do," she said, a faint smile beginning. "This should be a tale I haven't heard before."

Kina nodded, allowing herself to feel comfortable in telling it. She had plenty of practice already, and with each telling it seemed to grow a lot more interesting, even to herself.

Chapter Seven

The four continued their travel through the fields of Edan, distancing themselves from the towns and populous areas and trying to keep near the forests whenever possible. They had strayed too close to Gawthrain's men in the monastery, and no doubt the Duke had heard of what had transpired there. Daven reasoned that the Duke would put greater emphasis on their capture now, perhaps even to the point of throwing away his attempts at concealment of his intentions. It was one thing to be wanted as thieves, it would be quite different to be sought after by an entire kingdom.

Of their new companion, Kina noted that Nadia spoke often in sarcastic tones, but rarely with cruel intent to her words. She seemed to regard herself with a lot of self-loathing, an emotion that Kina felt she shared with the ancient malakh. She didn't, however, see why Nadia felt that way about herself. She moved easily over the uneven ground, stepping lightly and with a grace that denied belief. She had confidence in everything she did, and she was beginning to seem livelier as the days went by. It was only now that Kina realized that she would have been completely at ease by her side were it not for the strange dark symbols she could see circling the warlord. Kina no longer used the word 'witch' to describe Nadia. The definition didn't seem to apply here.

Daven remained distant to Nadia. The initial fiery hatred spent, he focused on his tasks in bitter silence whenever she was near. Lyle took the brunt of Daven's anger, but Kina noted that the older brother took it much the same as the taunting that was normally directed his way. A grunt, a glare, but she was beginning to realize that there was more to Lyle than perhaps even Daven realized. A puppet, Daven had said. No, Lyle was much deeper than some shallow foot soldier obeying orders without question. She had noticed it when he first spoke to Nadia. He seemed to understand something about her that Kina hadn't picked up on. She wished she knew what it was he saw, and what he was thinking about. As much as Lyle seemed to take in what went on around him, he revealed little about himself.

Herself, Kina remained quiet and listened to the others. Daven spoke to her of the trails they followed, and the arts of tracking he had picked up in the field. As experienced as she was at traveling, she had never been told what was required to be an effective tracker. She knew Drago had kept that information to himself, as a way of appearing stronger to his group. That Daven would share this information freely meant a lot to her.

Kina awoke one night to silent darkness. The ground was lit only by the stars in the moonless sky, the fire had long been extinguished to prevent it from being spotted. Something was different this night, however, and Kina felt a strangeness in the air. Alarmed, Kina sat up and took in her surroundings in the darkness. They had camped in a small opening within a wooded area, and while it offered them some protection, the trees looked dark and foreboding at night. The two brothers were still deep in sleep, Daven nearest to her. Of Nadia, there was no sign. Her bedroll remained untouched. She looked about warily, feeling nervous that the malakh would have left them alone so suddenly.

Kina quietly slipped away from camp, following her senses and trusting her instincts. She had traveled very little distance before she found Nadia sitting alone at the edge of the woods beneath one of the bordering trees. The small woman seemed at ease, though she spoke to herself in soft whispers that even with her cursed ears Kina could not make out. She was not at all certain the words were even spoken in a language she knew.

It was then she noticed that Nadia was not truly alone. Lighted glowing orbs the size of Kina's closed hand floated and danced around the small woman. Kina gasped at the sight, and even that small sound seemed enough to startle the tiny creatures. They moved tentatively before once more renewing their dance for Nadia.

Nadia didn't outwardly react to Kina's sound, but her voice spoke softly. "There is nothing to be afraid of, they won't harm you." It was an invitation, she realized, one she hesitated to take. She stepped slowly, cautious not to frighten the tiny creatures further.

"These are sprites," Nadia told her, holding out her hand to them, palm extended. Kina gaped in wonder as one of the tiny creatures floated down to nearly touch Nadia's hand. It shimmered and sparkled, a changing light that seemed to be composed of many hundreds of smaller ones.

"I've heard many stories," Kina admitted breathlessly, "but I have never seen a sprite before."

Nadia glanced Kina's way briefly, before returning her attention to the tiny sprite in her hand. "I find that surprising. One who has traveled these lands such as you have seen sprites at a distance at the very least." The malakh stared across the dark field in a way that suggested to Kina that she was remembering more than seeing. "Sprites are by far the most common of magical creatures. And the most social."

"They talk?" Kina whispered, awed by the tiny creatures.

Several danced toward her energetically.

"In their own way," Nadia answered. "They are drawn to magic, so they tend to cluster in large social groups."

"I've heard so much of them from legends. They used to be so plentiful that adventurers would often see and speak of them on their travels." Kina giggled as a sprite danced along her own outstretched hand. She couldn't feel anything touch her skin, but there seemed to be a warmth that centered beneath the tiny light.

Nadia made a strange grunting sound that sounded much like disgust. "Sprites are one of the few creatures that have not been hurt by the loss of magic in our world. Their numbers are much the same, even if fewer speak of them. The people fear them now, no longer understanding the world they live in." Nadia focused on Kina, a strange look on her face. "You said you have dealt with ghosts in your recent travels."

"Yes, in one of the earliest temples to Annasus."

"Yet these simple creatures draw such strong emotions from you?"

"Yes." Kina met Nadia's eyes. "Everything I've encountered has been too dangerous to get close to. When I was younger, the first creatures of magic I encountered were wraiths. Since then I have been wary of magic myself, though not fearful of it."

"Perhaps I begin to understand your attraction to Veran," Nadia commented while watching Kina's antics. "Be warned, while you may wish for divine intervention, often it comes with danger of another kind."

Strengthened by thoughts of how brave her companions were, Kina grinned confidently. "Danger does not frighten me."

"A bold statement," Nadia noted. She ducked her head low and put her pendant on. Kina blinked in surprise that she had not noticed that Nadia had been holding it in her other hand the entire time. Nadia touched it with her finger as if confirming that it did dangle from her neck before looking skyward. "If what you say were true, it would also be foolish."

Kina flinched before smiling apologetically. "I'm sorry, I meant only to be as brave as the company I keep."

"Without fear we would be unable to recognize the dangers in this world," Nadia scolded. Her response was harsh, but her posture seemed to relax as she watched the sprites circling steadily higher into the sky. Kina marveled at the way they seemed like distant stars in the sky.

"On the topic of dangerous," Nadia spoke in more amused sounding tones now, and Kina looked to her curiously. "I see you have taken a liking to Daven."

Kina thought the small woman was teasing, but she caught a more serious look in her eyes that suggested that there was a warning in her light tones. "Why would that be dangerous?" she asked without admitting to her hopes.

"Daven is an interesting man," Nadia said, perhaps catching some of Kina's own emotions. "Strong, handsome, charismatic even, when he's not brooding about. He has his own scars, however. Before you ask it, I do not know what burned his soul. I only recognize the signs. He is ruled by his emotions, and is often self-destructive. These are traits that he was not born into this world with. Life will not be easy for him. Or for those who choose to share in his life." Nadia smirked at Kina. "If all you want is just to bed him however..."

Kina squawked indignantly and shoved Nadia away. Immediately she froze, fearful of some kind of retribution from the warlord. Instead of violence she was greeted with laughter. She giggled at Nadia's laughter. For one so feared, she had a joyful sounding laugh with no menace within it. "I'll have you know," Kina said, "that I'm not that kind of woman."

"Perhaps," Nadia snickered. "Life needs to be enjoyed however. I would have him if he would have me. Just for a night."

Kina's amusement faded as she realized what Nadia was

admitting. The thought of them together made her stomach clench tightly. It angered her, it hurt. It was an emotion she was unused to having so little focus driving it that she was surprised by the power behind it. She stood to leave, no longer amused by the antics of the sprites. Kina regarded the woman and tried to bury the turmoil of emotion she felt inside. She chose not to say anything to avoid hinting that she was angry.

"Sit," demanded Nadia.

Stunned by her own actions, Kina sat submissively as she stared at the smaller woman. Her body just did as commanded without Kina's consent. The blackness closed in on Nadia, but it was not sustained and once more the symbols lessened and faded.

"What was that you just did?" Kina asked, her own voice demanding answers from the malakh.

"Nothing that you need worry about," Nadia returned, her gaze returning to the field. "The power of gods is not to be trifled with. You speak their names and carry a weapon forged for their kind. That is a boldness that would be rewarded with suffering in times past. Many humans were killed for far less." Nadia left her words hanging in the evening, either waiting for a response from Kina or for the depth of her words to sink in. Kina chose silence. She did not question such words from one who lived in those times, even if she was angry.

Once more Nadia began to speak, this time looking into Kina's eyes with a strange sadness. "I wonder what truths you think you know of their kind however, and I find myself curious as to why you would allow yourself to be swayed by them. Tell me what you think you know of them. Why do you give them power over you?"

Kina hesitated, not really wanting to stay and speak to her further but gradually relenting to her gaze. "When I was young I hoped for change, and when I heard mention of a Goddess of Change I secretly prayed to her for help. As I grew older, I learned from various stories about the gods of old. Even the new religions spoke of Veran. Still, I have always felt as though there was some watchful power that guided me. My life has been interesting, not the farmer's wife that was planned for me."

"Do not belittle the simple life," Nadia told her with a seriousness Kina hadn't expected. "It is by the back of the farmers that the rest of man is able to live as they do." Kina blinked as she recognized the similar sentiment that Daven had shared. Nadia shifted uneasily. "Nephrita, what do you believe you know of her?" Kina tried to understand the tone of Nadia's question. It seemed as though she were expecting an answer, almost demanding one, and Kina wasn't sure what it was she wanted to hear.

"Not much. Eldest of three daughters of Veran. Powerful, prideful, and prone to making rash decisions. I know she fought and lost against Annasus and I believe she remains imprisoned by the Gods of Light. I have heard she caused some trouble in the land before the coming of the Gods of Light, but there is not much to give weight to that."

"Trouble, right." Nadia nodded to herself. "Nephrita drew trouble to her like birds to the field. She did cause a lot of grief to the people of these lands, do not believe otherwise. Do not forget that her sword carries her power, and that your transformation is linked to it. You are lucky to look as you do. Her magic, uncontrolled, could have left you as anything."

Kina swallowed hard at the thought that she may have become something far worse. Nadia seemed to have a lot of knowledge regarding the ancient goddess. Perhaps it was her own long life that had allowed her access to such knowledge since Nadia would have been living in times before such knowledge was forbidden to the people.

"Nephrita had a temper like no other among the gods. There were none feared as much as she." Nadia grimaced unpleasantly.

"And what of her sisters, I wonder. I do not hear any stories of them in these lands any more. What knowledge do you have of them?"

Kina thought hard for a moment, combing her memories for what she knew of them. "I believe Laural was a patron of wild flowers," she said, though not with any certainty. "I've heard various descriptions of her appearance from legends and tales, but none agreeing on any one feature.

"Of Petra I know even less," she admitted to Nadia. "Mischievous, it was said, but there is little mention of why. She appeared less in the stories I've heard than even Laural. She doesn't seem to have played much of a role during the Time of Gods and Magic."

"No, I don't believe she did," Nadia agreed distantly. "It's amazing how names of such powerful lineage can be forgotten through time." There was an odd bitterness to her voice now, and a dark smile on her face. "Veran's power of change is two-edged. Even the Goddess of Change could not prevent the fall of her kind."

Kina thought about what Nadia said for a moment before calmly defending the goddess. "Veran does not control all of change. We all make our own choices in life and change how we view the world."

"Veran didn't welcome the change," Nadia growled. "She sent her daughters into battle to prevent it."

"I never saw reference of that," Kina admitted.

"Do not forget I was there." Nadia fixed Kina with a stare that seemed both threatening and powerful. Kina edged away from the warlord as she felt the power of the dark magics increase with the woman's anger. "I lived through those times. Those were battles this world has not seen the like of again since, not even through the great wars fought between Edan and Faneria. I do not need embellished and exaggerated stories to tell me what I witnessed with my own eyes."

Nadia stood, surrounded by her own dark emotions in an almost visual spectrum. "Tell me, do you seek to bring the lies back to this land?"

Kina pushed herself back to her feet and met the warlord's glare with ease that startled her. "I seek only enlightenment."

Nadia didn't react, but her eyes were filled with turmoil and raging emotions. The woman eventually turned away without further word, leaving Kina to her confusion. Apparently Daven was right, she thought to herself unhappily. Nadia was going to make life complicated. She sat down again, and tried to make sense of the emotions the other had stirred up within her. It was a long night, and Kina did not get much sleep.

When morning came, Kina returned to awareness abruptly with the sounds of hurried movement. She had no more rolled over when Daven called out her name in a frantic yet hushed tone that suggested that she move her tired body quickly without questions. Kina burst from her bedroll and gathered Vashnir before trying to settle her senses upon the unknown threat. Her hand rested on the pommel while she held the still sheathed blade with her other, ready to reveal it at a moment if required.

There was no sight of trouble, though she could see from the others that trouble was near. Lyle stood watchful as Daven and Nadia hurriedly broke camp in the morning mists. She hesitated a moment before strapping Vashnir to her side and quickly grabbed her cloak. She would be of more use gathering up her own scant belongings than keeping watch.

She did keep her ears open, however. Beyond the sounds of hurried movement from her friends she could hear voices. Distant and calm, but many voices. An army of voices.

"They must have made camp after we settled in," Daven guessed while shoving his bedroll haphazardly into his bag. He wasn't doing a very good job of it, but he kept pressing his weight upon it until he had it in deep enough to tie his small bag off.

"How can the southern army of Edan sneak up on you in the middle of the night?" Nadia snapped. "They were there before we made camp."

"Impossible," he remarked dismissively. "I scouted this camp myself."

"I fail to see your point," she returned darkly.

"I am one of the better scouts in the region, I'll have you know."

"The region must be numb from the neck up, then." Nadia answered.

Lyle clearly had enough and decided to stop the pair before their volume grew too loud. "Shut up, you fools," he hissed. His hand on the sword at his side served to emphasize the danger they were in. Daven and Nadia looked to each other and seemed to come to some silent agreement to conclude their argument another time. Kina pulled her cloak on and reluctantly pulled the hood up over her head, once more hiding her features beneath the protective shadows it provided.

Daven grabbed her by the arm, already equipped and ready for travel. "Time to go," he told her with an odd smile on his lips. He pulled her along, not giving her time to collect her bag. She looked over her shoulder to see Nadia grab it on the run, swinging it over her back in a single graceful arc without missing a stride. Lyle jogged along after, leading the horses and watching the trees.

"Daven, how did they sneak up on us?"

"By accident," he replied unpleasantly. "They don't know that we are near, else they would be more cautious not to alert us of their presence. Now is a time for quiet." He released her and sped up so that he was running ahead of her, drawing his own sword as he passed between the trees. Kina did her best to keep up without making too much noise.

A man in leather armor leaped out from cover beside Daven, swinging an axe in a deadly arc. Kina tripped and fell as she tried to come to a halt, tumbling to the ground. Her arms stung, but she quickly pushed herself to her knees. Daven was fighting, the axe wielder having been cut down, but it seemed three more soldiers took the man's place. Daven moved with confidence, easily holding his own against the soldiers.

The sound of horns bellowed out from near, and shouts followed. It would seem that their luck had finally run out. Lyle charged past her next, not pausing to help her up as he crashed into the line of soldiers. His sword drove one to the ground in a vicious downward blow that had been mostly blocked by a spear. He moved much like Daven did, only when he struck it sent the soldiers of Edan sprawling.

Nadia walked past Kina next, sliding her own sword free in a casual motion. She strode into battle without hurry or concern for her own life. The former warlord was truly fearsome, thought Kina as she watched. She showed no urgency, always moving just enough to dodge or parry a blow, but always connecting with her blade upon vulnerable flesh. The way she moved suggested that no matter how many men faced her, she would always be a single step ahead of each blow.

And Kina lay alone, sprawled on the ground while her friends fought an army for her. She growled at herself, and her uselessness. She would not allow them to die for her. She stood and drew the ancient sword and held it before her. Yet she hesitated. She was no fighter, and Daven's lessons seemed to vanish from her memories. She blinked in shock at her inability to remember what he had taught her. She could remember everything, but for the skills she needed to defend herself.

Daven laughed amidst the battle, ducking beneath a wildly swung spear. She watched him with hopeless need. She wanted so much to help him, and yet she knew there was nothing she would be able to do. She was more use to him back here where he would not be distracted by her.

"Veran," she whispered, not taking her eyes from the young traveler, "if you wish me to bring change to this world you will have to show me the way. Show me how I can protect my friends." She closed her eyes and tried to allow the goddess to show her what needed to be done. She saw nothing. She did hear a change in the battle, however. The sounds slowed, as though those embattled no longer wished to fight.

Kina opened her eyes, and was startled by a light glowing brightly from Vashnir as she held it before her. It shone as brightly as the sun briefly, pulsing in time with her own heart. She stared in amazement at it before looking to Daven for an explanation. He stared back with just as much confusion and perhaps more. There were soldiers standing near him, but they too stood still. Fear, she realized, kept the fight from renewing.

She smiled faintly as she realized that once more she was favored by Veran. "Thank you," she whispered. "I will use your gift." She whipped back her hood, revealing the monster she had become, and tried to glare at the soldiers of Edan who threatened her friends. She raised the sword and took a step forward, bluffing really, but with the support of the gods it was an impressive enough display.

"Leave," Kina said simply, her voice not overly threatening in tone, but her message was clear and understood. They were near breaking. All it would take was a little bit more and the entire group would rout. Nadia smirked at Kina and turned to face the troops again, two bloody swords swinging in her hands as she prepared to renew her assault.

"I am the bringer of death," Nadia told them, stepping forward to renew her fight. "Be gone from my sight or feel the wrath of the gods of old."

That did it, Kina thought. A few turned and ran, some dropping their weapons as they disappeared back into the woods. Their leaders tried to rally them, called to them to take up their swords once more, but they too were shaken by what they had seen. Nadia's swords sought those that foolishly remained before her. Another two fell in an instant and morale broke. Daven chased them into the woods, followed closely by Nadia. Lyle remained near, stepping back tiredly.

"How did you do that?" Lyle asked, sounding a little alarmed by the strangeness he had just witnessed.

"I asked for a little help," Kina told him, cradling Vashnir in her hands and bowing her head. She thanked Veran once more for the help before sliding the weapon away.

Lyle looked at her oddly before putting his own sword back in its scabbard. "Come. We should put some distance between us and the Duke's men."

Kina nodded, understanding what he meant. She collected her bag and Daven's own. Lyle collected the remaining bags. He gave her a quick glance to see that she was ready, and began a light jog that she could easily pace herself to.

Nadia was wrong, Kina thought to herself. Veran was worthy of her prayers. The goddess had saved her life again. Perhaps it was as Daven said. Perhaps she was indeed favored by the gods of old in some manner. To what purpose she could not begin to fathom, but it was not necessary that she understand. She merely had to retain her faith.

They passed through several open fields but Lyle always led her back to the trees. Kina respected his wishes for silence and focused only on keeping up. She was not as fit, and she did slow her pace often, but she never stopped moving. If her efforts impressed him she would never know, for he never so much as smiled at her. It was not a comfortable journey. She had felt more warmth from Drago's mercenaries than she felt from Lyle.

They made camp hours later as the sun began to set on the horizon. The silence held. She found herself thinking about Daven again, and Nadia as well. She found their presence comforting despite their flaws. It was the sound of their voices as they spoke to her that she enjoyed. Lyle had shown so much more depth with each of them, and yet with her he offered mostly silence punctuated by questions that left her more confused. It was frustrating to her, and without Daven's company she floundered.

"Why do you hate me?" she found herself asking. Her question seemed to startle Lyle nearly as much as the sound of her voice startled her. Lyle looked at her, frowning deeply and looking troubled by her question. He tossed the dry branch he was collecting in the direction of the firewood he had gathered.

"I do not hate," Lyle told her gruffly, though his expression seemed hurt somehow. "Hatred warps perception."

Kina stared unwavering at him. While an interesting outlook, she realized he was dodging the question she had asked. Now that she had spoken it, she was not willing to let it go so simply. Lyle frowned and brushed himself off with his hands.

"Are you so meek that you need my approval? You can be stronger than you show. Daven tries to shelter you from hard decisions, it is his way, but it does you no good. I feel you have been sheltered from much in your life." Lyle raised a hand to still Kina's rebuttal. "Yes, you have made many tough decisions, but you commonly choose silence when others are present, instead willing to follow when you know better. You are far more knowledgeable than the likes of Daven about what we may face; perhaps it is time for you to speak your mind on such subjects. Do not seek the approval of others; tell us what it is we should be wary of. My silence is but an invitation for you to take the lead."

"I could not lead the likes of you," Kina protested. "You're so much stronger than I."

"I will not argue further on this matter. Do not allow others to sway you from what it is you want."

"But," Kina began before stopping once more. She sighed as she saw the look on Lyle's face. It seemed he didn't understand her at all. She wasn't as strong as he thought she was. She was just a skinny little nobody that liked to play in the dirt.

Lyle gave an exasperated sound, clearly frustrated by her, and stalked off to collect more firewood. She watched after him, somewhat surprised by the fact he had left her so abruptly. It took her a moment longer to play his words over in her head to understand something new about him. Lyle saw her differently than any other man she had met so far. He believed she had some wisdom to offer, though obviously his faith was misplaced.

Kina frowned as she looked down at the gathered pile of dried wood. She knew she had some strength, never questioned that, but she had never thought beyond her experience in solving ancient riddles. The possibility that he could be right spilled more questions upon her. She had learned so much from her life with Drago, but the mercenary proved to be a poor model to judge by.

Her mind so fixated on the questions that he had raised, she didn't hear Daven and Nadia until they were nearly upon her. She started as they greeted her, almost missing that their tones were strangely at ease despite the fact that neither had seen her since the battle that morning. Her own emotions were not so muted.

"You're safe!" she proclaimed happily, burying the thoughts that Lyle had dragged to the surface.

"Of course," Daven responded with a smirk, while Nadia shot him an odd glance.

"Quite the rogue, aren't you?" Nadia retorted, before returning her gaze to Kina. "There wasn't much fight left in them after your little show spooked them. We merely chased a few of the braver ones a little before we slipped off the trail and tried to find the horses. Unfortunately for us, they found them first. Hopefully it will take them a while before they find our tracks."

"The season has been pretty dry," Daven noted. "The ground might be hard enough to hide some of our tracks, but if they look hard enough they will pick up our trail."

Kina grinned slightly, realizing that there was a change between the pair. "You seem to be getting along better now," she told them. Daven shrugged and looked away, clearly reluctant to admit that he was at least momentarily getting along fine with the warlord.

Nadia took the opportunity to add a little shot of her own at the thief. "One tends to relent a bit when one is saved repeatedly in battle."

"Hey!" Daven yelped, looking back at Nadia sharply. "It was just the once."

"I'm going to scout the area," Nadia told Kina, pointedly ignoring Daven. "I think we could all sleep better knowing that somebody competent confirmed that the camp was safe."

"Insufferable," Daven spat as the smaller woman left. Kina hid a grin at his display.

"Maybe I was right in allowing Nadia to accompany us?" she asked, hoping to prompt Daven into admitting that perhaps he was wrong.

"She has uses," Daven admitted, watching Nadia from where they stood.

"I'm glad you're safe," Kina told him. "I'm afraid I forgot all our lessons."

Daven's attention was instantly back upon her, one eyebrow raised questioningly. "You forgot?"

"I saw all those soldiers attacking and I could not bring myself to move. I was so afraid."

"You faced ghosts and wraiths, and you're afraid of that riffraff?"

"I'm afraid of the soldiers too," Kina admitted. "Though I shall fear the soldiers less when I'm human once more." Daven seemed to stand taller when she admitted her fears to him. He grinned in his roguish manor and rested his hand on the pommel of his sword.

"You have nothing to fear of them while I travel with you."

"I know," she told him, smiling slyly. Perhaps Nadia was not so wrong in speaking her mind about Daven. Perhaps she was being too cautious about her own feelings about him. She did want him, but the fear of rejection had stayed her. She missed his teasing words. He had not said the little scandalous things to her as he did prior to finding Nadia.

Still she hesitated, and the moment passed. Daven smirked at her and headed off to set up camp, leaving her to her thoughts and emotions. She watched him, disappointed in him for not seeing what she wanted, and disappointed in herself for not having the courage to say it for herself. She turned away and looked skyward with a scowl. With Drago it was never so difficult to understand what he wanted. Would Daven have wanted her if she looked human once more?

And there she was, back to thinking of herself as a monster. Kina growled at herself, and stalked away from the camp. She was no closer to a cure and it didn't seem she would ever be. She needed time to think. If Lyle was right, it changed so much.

It was dark before Kina returned to camp. By then she noted that the fire was already going and Lyle tended to it impassively. The bedrolls were laid out, but Daven and Nadia were absent. She wasn't sure whether or not to be relieved by the reprieve.

She wanted to be with Daven, that much was clear to her. It was a desire that burned deep within her. She wanted to stand by his side as they defeated Gawthrain. She wanted to see his face as they traveled across Edan. She wanted Daven as her own. It was jealousy that she felt deep inside her when she saw Nadia with him.

Of course, knowing this and being able to act on her feelings were far from being the same. She was still a strange mix of creature and man, and Daven seemed so far out of reach. It seemed impossible to her that she could see her fantasies come true.

Kina was not going to be held by her fears though. She had come to realize that if she could face the traps and monsters in this world, that she could face herself. She would not allow herself to become trapped within her own self-doubt.

There was something else she had come to realize. She was not so weak. Although she was not able to fight like her companions, she did possess certain abilities that they lacked. Certainly her ability to remember things was helpful, but it was limited in how she could put it to use. She did not possess great intellect to put her retained knowledge to use. What she did have, however, was the abilities her cursed form had provided. She had known that her hearing had become much more sensitive but she had yet to understand how such an ability could be useful. She had been using it subconsciously since she had changed and never understood it. Her appearance too could be used to her advantage. Clearly it made the average person uneasy, and while that was why she was unable to find peace, it meant that she also intimidated the very soldiers sent to retrieve her.

"Kina." Lyle's voice sounded uncertain to her, and he looked at her with a strangeness that seemed oddly misplaced on his face. "That is a peculiar smile," he told her.

She flashed a grin at Lyle. "Do I make you nervous?"

"If I did not already know you were harmless, Kina, I would be."

Kina shifted, tossing her cloak on the ground and rested her hand on the pommel of Vashnir much as Daven had earlier. She posed dramatically and continued to smile at him. "Are you not curious as to what I'm thinking?"

She managed to make Lyle look mildly amused. "Curious? Perhaps. I fear however that whatever insanity has claimed you may be contagious, so I must decline in asking." He pushed the burning log over with a charred branch.

Kina sniffed at his reaction, and relaxed her pose. "I've given some thought to what you said," she told him with finality. "I thank you for your advice."

He looked to her but said nothing. She couldn't even read his expression for what he might be thinking. It disappointed her, but at the same time did not surprise her that she could not draw more from Lyle. She satisfied herself with the memory of the momentary smile he had offered her.

"I will not be afraid," she told him, "to give my thoughts voice."

Lyle grunted, and returned to the fire.

"Perhaps you could care little for my opinions, but now you shall know them." She continued anyway, trying to draw him out. "Perhaps you will wish then that I would have remained silent?"

"Perhaps," he agreed gruffly.

"Well, perhaps then maybe you could teach me what Daven could not." Lyle started and looked at her suddenly, confused and very focused on her. "Perhaps you could teach me to wield this sword that I carry. I depend on the will of the gods to provide help to you, and yet you seem most vocal about how little I need to know about defending myself."

Lyle's eyes narrowed sharply and he shifted where he sat. "I speak only that a young woman such as yourself should not have a need to take the lives of others."

"And if I have such a need? Does the Duke not seek me out through the use of his very armies?"

"It takes more than a few nights of training, girl. We have studied war for much of our lives. You think Daven gifted? He learned the use of weapons since the day he could hold a sword.

We are not some riffraff from the edge of civilization. You know nothing of battle, and it would be best that you remain ignorant of such matters."

She stood stunned by his outburst, momentarily deflated as she watched Lyle return to the fire. He looked both angry and embarrassed to her, and she wondered if he had meant to be as forceful as he was. Clearly it seemed that Lyle believed firmly that she should not know how to fight, and perhaps she had insulted him in some way. She was not beaten into submission like a meek little maiden.

"I don't seek to learn all that it is you have come to know. I don't wish to remember the faces of those lives I take. I do, however, need to defend myself. I am not a princess to be locked in some tower and protected, sir knight. I have fought to protect myself in the past, and while I am not proficient in any form of combat, I have killed." She looked at him tearfully as she recalled the memories of Loor. She no longer felt a monster for defending herself, but she didn't enjoy the memories of killing the mercenary. "I will carry his face with me to the end of my days. Do you remember so clearly? I still see the faces of those you dispatched this morning, and those that Nadia left on the stairs of the monastery. Do not think I take battle lightly. Do not ever think that."

The hardness to Lyle's expression faded and he looked at her with sorrow. "That is why I will not teach you," he told her simply. "What you have witnessed in your life haunts you still. For your sake, I do not wish more blood on your hands."

Kina looked at him hard, wiping her eyes bitterly. "And if that blood should be mine?"

"It will not," Lyle declared. He looked as though he had more to say but Kina would not allow his hypocrisy. He did not see the truth in his own words earlier.

"Why? Because you will protect me? Is this not what you were going to say? You spoke earlier of Daven sheltering me from decisions, but perhaps you too are guilty in this. Know this, I do not wish to fight but I don't want for others to die for me."

"And we willingly defend you because that is your honest wish." He raised his hand to still her protest. "But, I see your point as well. I will train you, for as long as you wish. Do not delude yourself into believing that this will mean you can defend yourself. It may take many months before you might reach the level of skill that even the most novice of soldiers has."

She wiped her eyes again, and nodded. "I understand. Thank you."

"Do not thank me," he retorted. He shook his head before looking to the fire in silence.

She smiled, though she felt only a faint glimmer of relief rather than joy at her victory. It had certainly been draining on her. She wondered if she had enough strength left for her next battle. "Where is Daven?"

"I do not know," Lyle scoffed. "Do not concern yourself with him."

She paused, and her head cocked slightly to the right in an unconscious attempt to hear the thief. She grinned as she could hear his voice distantly. She turned to leave, but Lyle's voice called out after her.

"Kina," he said almost sadly. "He is not worth your efforts."

She said nothing and continued away from camp. Despite Lyle's misgivings, she hoped Daven would listen. She needed to give voice to her feelings while she still felt the courage to do so. The darkness was of little hindrance to her search. She was able to see enough of the trees to avoid tripping over the uneven terrain held firm by their thick roots. She needed only to listen to Daven speaking softly and she would be able to discover him like any other treasure she had put herself to finding.

"Daven," she called out as she neared him, forcing herself to speak her mind quickly. "I want to... oh." She stopped, her feet suddenly fixing themselves upon the ground so suddenly that she had to steady herself against the nearest tree. Her mouth moved to say more, but even she didn't know what. She focused on breathing and took a step backwards away from the sight that she had found.

"Kina!" Daven rose from where he was laying, sitting up next to Nadia suddenly. She could not see the look on his face despite the fact she could clearly see the scars on both his body and that of the warlord he had despised not long ago. She could see that the dark shadowy signs indeed covered every part of her body, they flashed brightly as the she sat up and focused in a way that suggested that she was ready to fight. Nadia's words came back to Kina with shocking clarity. She had wanted Daven as well. And so it seemed, she had him.

Kina turned and ran back into the woods. She ran as hard as she could, but unlike Drago, she could not escape this night. She ducked into the hollow of a tree and sat down within, trying to keep herself silent. She didn't have the energy to run further. But she didn't want to be found.

Lyle's voice joined in with Daven's cries, but she shut them out. She cried softly to herself and fought the feelings of betrayal alone.

Morning came, and Kina awoke within the tree feeling stiff and parched. She ran her fingers through her hair and knocked large pieces of bark which had become knotted within the reddish strands. Remembering the vision the previous night had shown her was the worst. Kina buried her face in her hands and fought the urge to cry once more. She had waited a day too long to declare her feelings to Daven, and she had lost him because of it.

There was a sound in the woods. One which could have been a bird, if a very large one. Kina could hear the compression of air beneath wings as they beat hard. She frowned and focused now, trying to distance her thoughts from her senses. She could hear, what she thought to be, humming. A voice humming an odd song as an elderly man hiked through the woods. Despite the slanted morning light, Kina noted the familiar garb and remembered the gait well. The blind man from the tavern. The trees that hid them from the eyes of Gawthrain's men were seemingly little trouble for the likes of a blind man. Kina edged herself gently over the roots as she tried to get a better look at the strange old man. He had not seen her yet, but it was obvious the way he was picking his way through the forest that he was tracking them.

The blind man stepped carefully, moving around troubling roots and brush almost as though he could see them. Of course, Kina had seen his eyes and knew them to be sightless. Even then, however, she recalled that he moved well for somebody disabled. Once more she felt uncomfortable by his presence in ways she did not understand. How was it he had found them? Even with eyesight, they had been dodging an entire army for weeks.

"Kina!" She froze where she lay, refusing to take so much as a breath as the blind man paused in his approach. Daven, of course, had seen it necessary to call out her name. It was reckless and she found herself remembering her travels with him in a different light now. Lyle was right. Daven seemed incapable of thinking beyond the moment. No wonder he sought solace in worshiping Destine. Without planning, he believed whatever happened could be blamed on fate.

Her attention returned to the blind man as he smiled to himself and picked up his pace up the hill. What magic allowed for him to see without eyes? To find what no others could? She dipped her head lower to avoid whatever eyes were cast in her direction.

Daven's voice called out her name once more, this time causing neither her nor the blind man any hesitation. It would seem that they had both made up their minds about what they were about to do. She could hear Daven approaching, his feet avoiding much of the vegetation but still brushing against some of the thicker foliage. The light sounds he made would have been missed by her before, but she was getting to know her new body. Faith in her hearing, and knowing the sounds that she heard, Kina could now recognize the sounds and judge how far away they were. Daven was fairly well skilled in avoiding detection, and while not attempting to be silent he still instinctively avoided placing his feet on twigs and leaves. An odd scenario for a man who currently gave away his position by calling her name.

She felt no guilt in remaining silent. He was not alone, and the gentle strides that followed him were not the heavy steps of his brother. Nadia was with him. Sure enough her voice carried through the wood calmly. "Daven, relax. She won't have gone far."

"She has not been one to wander off. She didn't return last night. I hurt her." Daven said with a disagreeing tone. "Since I joined Kina's path it would seem fate has been leading us along. I will not allow her to face the Duke alone. Kina!"

"It's not fate. Destine has no power in these lands," Nadia responded, invoking the name of the Goddess of Destiny.

"I disagree. The old ones have merely been silent."

"Heretical thoughts, young adventurer," spoke a third voice. Kina identified it quickly as the blind man. "Most in this land would take exception to such statements."

Daven tensed, but Kina saw a different reaction from Nadia. There was the briefest of hesitation before she grinned in a manner more suited for the insane. "Garm, where are you?"

"Right here," the blind man answered, stepping forward into the opening. Kina shifted behind the branches so that she could see, but Garm's face remained hidden to her. "I see the prisons did not break you, pet."

"It wasn't that long," she answered in an oddly proud way.

"Just a few years of solitary added to the centuries of loneliness. Thank you for the rescue."

The blind man stood still, his expression unchanging. "It seemed a good idea."

Nadia took a step forward, but Daven grabbed her arm fiercely, pulling her back away. Kina frowned at his possessiveness. That should have been her standing next to Daven, not the warlord from Tanara.

"You will let go of me," Nadia demanded, not attempting to forcefully remove herself from his grip but instead using her voice alone to cause the separation. The coldness of her reaction to his protectiveness set off alarm bells in Kina's mind. As Daven released her she calmly stepped forward and put more than an arms breadth of distance between herself and Daven. She had not seen such forcefulness in Nadia. Except two nights previous when Nadia had ordered Kina to sit. She found herself thinking about that memory and wondering again why her body had reacted so quickly to the command.

"Ahh, so once more it seems your true self comes to the surface. That is the woman I fell for."

Nadia continued her slow graceful stride unhurriedly, showing no reaction to Garm's revelation. Daven meanwhile tensed, and Kina wondered if he would draw the sword he carried at his side. It seemed that her own jealousy was being reversed upon Daven. She worried that there would be violence, and was startled by part of her feeling that Daven deserved it. She tried to avoid thinking about Daven by focusing on the blind man.

"I am not to be toyed with," Nadia stated in a voice that seemed to echo. Her accent had changed subtly, one which Kina was not familiar with. She wondered if it was an intentional slip by Nadia. "What we had is gone."

"A loss," Garm remarked. The old adventurer sounded truly sorry for the loss. "You could have come with me."

"And become all that I hate," she retorted fiercely. "Never. I will not have the people of Tanara suffer for my actions. You however, the last I saw of you was shortly before Edan mobilized against us."

Garm shrugged. "Luck of timing,"

"You self-serving, cold-hearted, son of a wraith. You did not send Kina to me on your own well wishes. Why did you do it?"

"The girl was said to be holding the sword of Chaos, and you ask why I send her to you?" Nadia fixed him with a look of disbelief. He sighed and shrugged again. "I needed you to confirm it was authentic, Pet. Best way to do that was to dangle it under your nose and see if you would come looking for your sister."

"She should remain locked up. I care not about finding her."

"Ah, but you see, that is where we disagree. I have use for her where I no longer have use for you." He moved fast, faster than Kina thought possible and clearly faster than Nadia had expected. There was a look of stunned surprise as Nadia gripped the knife now protruding from her stomach. Kina hesitated, undecided whether to go charging recklessly to Nadia's aid, or to remain safely hidden from an obviously powerful foe.

"Nadia!" Daven yelped, racing forward.

Garm grabbed the amulet from Nadia's neck and ripped it free. "Your sister should be plenty more cooperative, once the spell is completed," Garm said in parting. "Sorry Pet." He took a step back, and disappeared from sight. Nadia stumbled a moment before collapsing to the ground and laying on her back. Kina hesitated a moment before deciding to rush in to Nadia's aid as well. She had no more than raised to her knees before she felt the cold edge of a blade at her throat.

"Hello Kina," Garm's voice greeted dangerously. "I need that sword."

She gritted her teeth and thought fast for a way out of this predicament. Unfortunately, she couldn't think of any options. Reluctantly she drew Vashnir from her side and the blind man snatched it away from her. The blade slipped away from her throat and she heard him back up a stride from her.

"Mortals should never play with such toys," he commented. Kina turned, but Garm was already gone. The sword, which carried all hope of a cure, was gone as well. She sat there despondent, so preoccupied with her curse that she forgot about the others. It wasn't until she heard Daven yelling for his brother that Kina returned to reality.

"I'm fine, you idiot!" Nadia protested, holding her hand to the wound. "Find Kina!"

Anger forgotten by the tone in her voice, Kina burst from her cover and returned to the group at a run. Daven and Nadia each looked surprised to see her, but they asked no questions. Kina kneeled in front of Nadia and looked at the blood seeping out between her fingers fearfully.

"What can I do?" she asked, looking helplessly at Daven.

"The sword," Nadia said with a grimace. Her expression fell once Kina met eyes with her. "He got the sword. Damn him." Nadia shifted, pulling herself from Daven's grip and started to get up. Both Kina and Daven began to protest but she stilled them with a cold look filled with power.

"Garm knew that wouldn't be enough to kill me, he just needed to slow me down long enough to get the sword." She flung the bloodied dagger at a tree, sinking the blade fully into the trunk. Kina blinked in surprise at the display of strength. "Gawthrain must be close to calling Nephrita back into this world."

"Why should we fear that?" Daven asked, though it didn't seem to Kina that he believed otherwise.

"Because Garm knows the control spells placed on me," Nadia remarked darkly. "If he passed that information on to Gawthrain they could attempt to control her the same way."

"I don't understand," Kina stammered, still staring at the blood on Nadia's hands. "Are you talking about the spells that cause those black symbols around you? Those spells couldn't work on a goddess, could they? Who is Garm?"

Nadia stopped moving, and looked ill. She met Kina's gaze almost reluctantly. "I have not lied to you, but I have misled you." Nadia motioned to the wound in her stomach which no longer seemed to be bleeding quite as bad. "The mercenaries I traveled with were more than what they seemed. We were outcasts of the fallen gods. Followers, champions and even those with the blood of the gods flowing in their veins. What we tried to do at Tanara was something more, yes, but I will not say what. One of our objectives, though, was to locate an old spell book and prevent it from falling into the hands of somebody like Gawthrain."

"So Garm is one of the gods?" Daven asked, his body tensing as he looked about the trees warily.

"He does have such power, but he is not of the gods."

Kina came to the truth faster than Daven had. "But that would make you connected to the gods in some way."

"In some way," Nadia acknowledged, using Kina's own words. "Do not misunderstand, I have no wish to see their return to this land no more than I'd wish to see the Gods of Light walk these fields. Gawthrain had sent his men into the ruins of Wyecroft in search of the spells he intends on using now. I could not allow for that to happen."

"It would seem you have failed," said Lyle's deep voice. Kina jumped. She had not heard him approach. He stood not far off, apparently content to stand at a distance and listen to what was being said rather than approach and chance interrupting.

Nadia looked angry at first, but she held her tongue while she reigned in her emotions. "So it seems. I suspect that Garm has something to do with that as well. There are very few with knowledge of these spells that still live. Being able to twist the mind of a god is not something that goes unnoticed. My pendant contained half a page from the spell book from Tanara."

"I still don't understand. A god would be more powerful than any magic a human can conjure."

"Kina," Daven interrupted gently, "I think Nadia is a goddess."

"What?"

Nadia shifted uneasily before standing up and taking a few easy strides. She flicked her hands sending droplets of blood into the soil before turning to face Kina directly. "I have not always been known as Nadia. I was once known as Petra, daughter of Veran."

Kina gasped and backpedaled away from Nadia. She looked again, noting that she seemed to be showing no more signs of discomfort from her wounds, and was already walking without holding her hands to staunch the flow of blood. While amazing, and beyond what Kina thought of as human capabilities, it was not what Kina had pictured as godlike powers.

"Kina, not all gods have the supreme power. My father was human, as I said before, and yes, he was a king of Wyecroft so long ago. I spent much time in his realm rather than laying waste to the non-believers. I did not fight when the Gods of Light came to this land, so I was not defeated."

Daven looked slightly unnerved by the revelation of who she was, but remained true to his impulsive ways. "Why was that? You look as though you would enjoy a good fight," he said, tempting another fight.

"Why should I fight for their reasons? I was never one of them. All they think of is themselves."

Daven didn't back down. "And that makes you different, how?"

"Because I would rather that the people be allowed to live without being manipulated."

"You manipulated us! You killed armies!" Daven snapped

back, raising his voice with his anger.

Nadia opened her mouth to return in kind and she looked as though she was going to use fists as well as words, but Lyle intervened. "While I believe Kina is learning much from this argument, I must admit I have had my fill of it. What has come to pass cannot be undone. Gawthrain now has Vashnir and apparently the second half of a spell to control a goddess. I trust I am not the only one that sees where this leads."

Daven and Nadia both looked from Lyle to each other before almost as one taking a step back from each other. Even Kina realized the implications. They had failed.

"I'm sorry," Kina offered, bowing her head. "It's my fault that the sword is gone."

"I doubt that," Nadia responded darkly. She turned to Daven. "How did you know?"

"Know what?"

"How did you know that Garm was allied against us?"

"Lucky guess," he said with a maddening grin.

"Great," Nadia muttered.

"What next?" Lyle asked, his voice sounding grim.

"Brighton," Kina spoke with certainty.

"I suppose hitting him where he lives makes sense," Daven responded thoughtfully.

"It is more than that," Nadia noted. "Brighton was built upon the doorway the Gods of Light used to enter this world. He will want to be as close to that portal as he can get. The closer he is, the easier the summoning will be."

"What is this doorway?" Kina asked. "I have never heard of it."

"Not surprising. The legends go that the Gods of Light came into this world and struck down the Gods of Time. They never say where those of the Light came from." Nadia stated. "The gateway was not an object that was well understood even before the Gods of Light stepped through it. It existed before the Gods of Time."

To Kina's ears this sounded wonderful. It was a piece to an ancient mystery that the temples refused to teach. Perhaps they themselves had long forgotten where their gods had come from. She had dozens of questions for the goddess, but she was unable to find the words fast enough to ask them.

"Nadia, the control spells. Can they use them to control you?" Lyle asked, leading the conversation down another path.

Nadia shook her head. "No. They would need to bind me to them, and they have nothing to bind me with. It is not my sword they have."

"It was your pendant," Daven pointed out.

"Garm has no reason to bind me."

"Who does have control over the spells on you? Garm?" Lyle seemed to be on to something. Kina realized belatedly that if somebody could control Nadia, it could be their strongest ally could become a powerful enemy.

"You will forgive me if I refuse to answer that question. And Garm would not control me."

"He just shoved a knife in your gut," Daven argued. "It doesn't appear that your friendship means that much to him."

"And if he wanted me dead he would not have stopped there. That lizard is plotting something, but I am too small for his games. Had Garm wanted to control me he would never have let me take half that spell with me. The deal was he took the book to safety, I take the page. Suffice to say, we should not delay getting that sword back. If you think I am powerful, you will not like what a full blooded goddess under the control of a warlord like Gawthrain will do."

"Brighton will be well defended. The walls are near impenetrable," Lyle noted.

"I can take care of the walls," Nadia remarked dismissively.

"And wake up the entire kingdom in the process," Daven

argued.

"The walls will not be a problem," Kina answered distractedly.

"What?" Daven grabbed her by the shoulder roughly. "What was that?"

"What?" she asked back, startled back into the present. She wondered if she had made a mistake by speaking up.

"The walls, what was that about the walls?"

"The people believe they are safe behind the walls, but I've seen plenty danger that would not be slowed by them."

"How?" Lyle asked, his normally gruff voice sounding strained by his curiosity.

"The town has grown much since the walls were made. There are numerous blind spots where the guards cannot see. Underground there are tunnels and crypts that lead unknown lengths beyond the city." She listed quickly, adding, "Also the walls are old and poorly made, a good army would hardly be held off by them."

"The legends of Brighton," Daven chuckled. "Impenetrable walls, indeed."

"I do not think finding Gawthrain will be as simple as slipping over the walls undetected," Lyle pointed out.

"With magic feared, he'll have to summon Nephrita from a place out of sight," Daven noted.

"Near to the actual gateway," Nadia reminded.

"Underground," Daven sighed.

Lyle leaned against a tree, his body looking relaxed despite the tension in his face. "He will have guards at the entrance to whatever hole he is hiding within, but I doubt that any of his soldiers would be permitted entrance. Word of tampering with magic would destroy the loyalty he has built with his men."

"If he is serious about claiming Edan as his own, he won't risk that," Daven agreed readily.

"If he is successful in controlling Nephrita it will not only be

Edan that he will take," Nadia added. She inspected her ruined tunic, and the stained hole unhappily. "However, as was bluntly pointed out earlier, an army does not concern me."

Lyle and Daven looked to each other uncertainly.

Chapter Eight

The journey back to Brighton was a tense event, but strangely without the danger provided by the Duke's scouts. There were no signs of soldiers as they headed north into the heart of the Mad Duke's domain. Word must have reached them that they had achieved their victory. Vashnir was now in the hands of their lord, and a mere four travelers were of little concern to the victorious warlord.

They traveled in the open so that they could cover more ground, but they did so near enough to the trees whenever possible. They needed to make up as much time as they could and with the horses gone, they shared the load of bags and left what they could spare behind. The bags grew heavy as they continued their march northward, and their legs grew tired, but they dared not rest while there was daylight left to them.

There was little joy shared between them now. The evenings were uneasy as they settled in to rest, and Kina realized that she was in the middle of it. Daven remained stiff near her, always ready to offer help, but always distant or apologetic. He was no longer the man she had come to know. This stranger she journeyed with was not somebody she wished to know. Let Nadia tend to his needs. Kina sat nearer to Lyle when they camped and remained silent unless pressed for an answer directly.

Clear though their path was, it still took many days to retrace their steps and return to the city of Brighton. Kina had pushed hard before with Drago, but never with the same sense of urgency. When the walls of Brighton were finally within sight, she was relieved more for the moment of rest while the company decided their course. The city was of course well defended. The impenetrable walls of Brighton were perhaps not as strong as legends told, and it was clear Gawthrain did not share his people's faith in them. His army was amassed outside the gates, camped out and waiting. There were guards high in the towers, ever watchful, and mounted scouts trotted beyond the perimeters of the camp. It was an intimidating sight that made Kina's tired body feel even heavier. The army had not come as a surprise to her companions, but for her to see the vast numbers of soldiers standing between them and the city was a frightening return to reality. Nobility did not maintain power on their generous nature, and as Gawthrain had no such generosity he required many more soldiers.

"Well, there are the walls. Now what?" Nadia asked, her voice sounding maddeningly calm to Kina's ears.

Daven grinned maniacally, casually shifting his posture. "Now we defeat the army, stop the evil ceremony and thereby thwart the Mad Duke's plans." He ignored the resulting looks his response generated.

After a moment's hesitation Nadia laughed darkly, breaking the moment of awkward silence that had gripped them. "I like it. The plan lacks detail, but I like it."

Lyle snorted.

"Let's hear your idea," Nadia challenged.

"Retreating back to Faneria," Daven responded, looking back over his shoulder at his elder brother. "But you and I both know that we need to stop Gawthrain now."

"A charge of the king's own would have been nice." Lyle

shifted, and looked to the city. "Do we know where the Duke summons this evil from?"

Eyes looked first to Nadia before settling on Kina. She looked at the three uncertainly before she realized that they expected her input on the matter. "I've only been in a few of the caves beneath Brighton. I saw nothing that would suggest the work of gods."

"You have seen more than we have," Nadia told her firmly. "I may know it's down there, but I have never ventured into those caves. My kind is not welcomed."

"Where do we need to be?" Lyle asked Kina, moving directly to the point.

"I always entered from points within the walls," she said unhappily, but she knew of one good passage outside the walls. "However, I did exit near those trees to the west of the camp." She pointed to the familiar cluster of trees.

"I don't like the approach," Nadia commented, looking at the soldiers near it and the lack of adequate cover approaching the area.

"It's better than climbing the walls," Daven argued. "What of the tunnel?"

"Dangerous," Kina said firmly. "But passable. I can take us into the city through it."

"Hey," Daven said, interrupting Kina suddenly and looking to Nadia intently. "You're a goddess of old. You know Fate, right? Maybe you know why she hates me?" Kina shook her head. Even now it seemed he wasn't going to take her serious.

"Destine?" Nadia looked confused. "Not that I know Destine, but she was not the type to take interest in a single being."

"She does. She torments me daily. She must hate me. Why else do I keep finding myself in these situations?"

Lyle snorted and rolled his eyes. Nadia feigned deep thought before giving what Kina thought to be a well worded answer. "Because you're an idiot."

"That is an ugly storm brewing," Lyle interrupted, his voice gruff and hinting to unseen stress. Daven and Nadia both looked up at the dark clouds which seemed to be blowing in from all directions at once. Kina had never seen such patterns before.

"That is no mere storm," Nadia noted, her tone dropping all traces of mirth she had shared with Daven moments before. "That is a divine warning to those who would involve themselves with dark powers. We run short on time."

The winds were indeed picking up, and there was a chill in it that suggested rain was not far off. Nadia wrapped her arms around herself tightly and shuddered slightly. "We need to hurry." She looked up at the clouds, lost to her memories and the ghosts of the past.

Lyle was the only one of them with the nerve to ask the question. "Should we expect divine intervention?"

"I hope not," Nadia responded. "It would be best if we put an end to this insanity before it comes to that. We should either use Kina's cave or charge through Gawthrain's army now." Nadia looked to Daven and Lyle for an answer, and Kina noted the uncertainty in their own postures. It was not a hard decision and they quickly agreed upon Kina's subterranean entrance.

"Leave the bags. Don't draw your weapons until needed. And lose the armor," Daven ordered his brother. "It will reflect the sunlight." He was already putting his bags on the ground and unloading much of his belongings.

"Not much sunlight left," Lyle grumbled, looking up at the sky, but he was already unstrapping it. Kina hesitated and started to likewise unburden herself. She would not need for her bedroll underground. Anything that could be spared was left behind.

Nadia looked to Lyle and shrugged. "Give me a few minutes before you move, but follow in my footsteps. I will find the best path. Daven, I need your bow." Without hesitation the younger brother tossed her his bow and his quiver of arrows. Nadia studied the weapon quickly before nodding with satisfaction. "A good weapon."

"I should hope so. The high and mighty Earl of Marrows was proud of it," he responded, giving his brother a dark look.

"I'm sure that is an interesting tale, but I shall have to hear that story another day." Nadia nodded to Kina and made to leave, but hesitated before she made much more than a few strides. She turned back again, looking concerned. "Kina. You have been unarmed since Garm stole Vashnir. That's too long. You will need to arm yourself this day."

"I wouldn't be able to use any you could spare," Kina responded, realizing that Nadia was trying to reopen the paths of communication that had been severed between them. The look in her eyes betrayed concern for Kina's safety.

"Should we survive this, I will be certain to teach you how to defend yourself, girl."

Lyle exhaled loudly, a sound of disgust that shocked both Kina and Nadia. "Not you too," he said angrily. "I begin to wonder if Kina does have some spiteful edge to her character. She has managed to convince us all to train her."

"Had you two done what you have said, we wouldn't need to watch out for her," Nadia returned harshly.

Kina stepped toward Nadia, taking her between the goddess and Lyle. "Please, you need not worry about my sake, but if you would have a knife to spare, I would accept that."

"A knife?" Her companions looked confused by her words once more.

"It has plenty of uses beyond drawing blood. I lost mine during my escape through the Darkwood."

Nadia bent over and pulled a small knife from her boot. She flipped it through the air once, catching it by the flat of the blade and offered the handle to Kina.

Kina nodded, and gently took the blade from Nadia's hand.

"Thank you." She gave it a quick glance, memorizing its stark appearance at a glance before sliding it into a pouch on her belt. It was not as fancy as her dagger had been, nor quite as long, but it seemed fitting for her new life. She was not some ornament on Drago's arm any longer. "Shall we be off?"

Nadia shook her head, and grinned in a manner most unlike any she would have expected of a goddess. "Have some patience, girl. There are more than enough soldiers for us all." Nadia looked to Daven and Lyle much more firmly. "Wait for my signal. Keep low and try not to draw attention." With that, the small woman turned and ran, hunched over so that she was lower to the ground. Kina watched her go as the brothers returned to readying themselves.

Lyle cleared his throat, and Kina turned to meet his gaze. His eyes clouded with emotions while his face remained cold. "I have followed you this far because we shared the same path. Today I follow because it is what I want." He held her gaze for a moment longer, and almost reluctantly he added, "May whatever spirits that guide you protect you."

"Very poetic," Daven's sarcasm and playful laugh earned him another grunt from his brother. Lyle shrugged off the last of his armor from his shoulders and gently lay it out on the ground. The pair had eliminated any remaining weight they carried, laying it in small piles in the long grass.

Lyle stared hard at her for a moment as if in conflict with himself over whether he should speak or hold his tongue. It seemed this moment in time Lyle was more apt to speak to her than usual. "If any of us should fall, do not turn back. You need to find that chamber."

Kina swallowed hard, realizing what he meant. She had not considered the possibility that any of the others could fall on this day. She understood now what Lyle really meant. They would put their lives at risk to make certain that she could find that chamber.

She had been guided by three of the most powerful warriors she had yet to meet, and today they looked to her. Kina relented to Lyle's demand, and nodded slowly.

"Hold," Daven's voice was tense now, and he stopped moving entirely as his eyes searched the sky. Lyle likewise tensed, and Kina grew wary as she too looked in the direction that Daven now stared. "I thought I saw an arrow fly."

Kina's skin tingled unpleasantly and she shivered against the cooling winds. This was pressure she was unused to. She had never needed to find a lost passage under such a deadline before. And never had so much depended on her finding her way.

"There," Daven said, and Kina's head lifted upward to the sky. An arrow seemed to fall from the heavens, and it burned brightly against the darkening sky. A streak of flame across the sky. It came down amidst the soldiers in the camp and instantly the tents were ablaze. Soldiers scurried about, seeking to contain the fires and tame the horses. A good distraction and an obvious signal.

Kina looked to the two brothers for their intentions, and belatedly moved to follow them as they had set out across the fields. She hurried along, low to the ground, as she listened to the calls for action from the camp. The soldiers would not see them. With the ever darkening storm and now the burning light of the fire amidst them, the soldiers were well occupied on this day.

But there were other dangers to come.

They regrouped with Nadia closer to the trees and the caves. The woman that awaited them looked very much like a warrior of legend, though somewhat shorter. Nadia stood with the bow in one hand and an arrow in the other, looking relaxed but wary. The dark enchantments were in full force now, however, and Kina kept her distance despite herself.

Daven and Lyle seemed unaffected and showed little reluctance in approaching Nadia. Daven even grinned and looked unconcerned by the forces of magic which were rapidly coming to focus around them. Kina shared Lyle's uneasiness.

"The entrance isn't far," Kina told them. "We can get into Brighton through there, but it will take time."

Nadia nodded and looked to the fires she had set. "We are close, Kina. Much closer than I would have expected." The demigod closed her eyes and seemed to drift away. "The ceremony is nearer to us than those walls. We must be quick." Her eyes snapped open again and she looked at Kina pointedly. "We have used up all the time we have to spare just to get here." She looked to Daven and Lyle the same way as if pushing that point to them as well.

Kina made to lead the group forward, but Nadia stayed her with a quick hand motion. "I go first," Nadia said simply, giving Kina a hard look. The small woman ran ahead, keeping low to the ground as she moved. Kina didn't wait long and was quickly on Nadia's heels. Daven and Lyle followed her, spacing themselves apart as they ran.

Strangely, Kina began to compare the situation to those she had experienced with Drago and his band. She had witnessed battles before, but she had never strayed near to the fight let alone take part in one. Now, as she ran to the cover of the trees, she realized that she was playing a large role in this one.

There weren't many trees around the cave entrance but as Nadia entered between them she vanished from sight. If it was a trick of the light or Nadia used some magical power that allowed her to disappear Kina did not know.

Kina felt her body grow cold and she stumbled. She regained her footing quickly enough, but something had changed. Momentarily she was afraid that the summoning had been completed but her mind refused to allow that thought. She came to a stop and got low to the ground. Perhaps it was too late, but she trusted her instincts now. They were not alone any more.

Before Daven and Lyle had reached her, she spotted Garm amidst the trees. He was waiting for them. He had allowed Nadia passage into the woods but seemed to stand in their way. Fearfully, Kina lay flat hoping that she wasn't seen. Lyle kneeled next to her as Daven passed by at a slower, more cautious pace. "What do you see?" Lyle asked, his voice gruff but open.

"Garm," Kina told him, raising her head and looking straight at the strange blind man still among the trees. She could feel Lyle tense next to her. "Nadia warned us not to fight him. What do we do?"

Lyle frowned, and looked to the trees uncertainly. It was clear this was not something he had an answer for either. Reluctantly he nodded to himself, and drew his sword. "We do what we must." He stood openly, challenging their hiding adversary. Daven noted the change in his brother and likewise drew his blade and stood. Kina looked at the pair as they stood silently together.

"Show yourself to us, Garm. You can no longer play your games with us."

Lyle's voice drew the strange man from the trees, though he appeared with a smile. "I have yet to begin with you," he said in good humor. "I am well and above the likes of any mere mortal. Put away your sword and leave this place."

"You pretty much invited us, Garm," Daven remarked back, smirking slightly. "Do you stand against us?"

"If I must," Garm remarked. "I shall not let you pass."

Daven and Lyle looked to each other briefly, and Kina noted the look of concern that passed between them. Lyle didn't look to her, but he spoke to her softly. "When he is occupied, make for the trees. Find Nadia. She will protect you now. We will follow if we are able to."

"I understand," she answered, lowering herself further into the grass.

Daven charged first, raising his blade as he ran at the seemingly unprepared blind man. Lyle moved quickly to follow, obscuring Kina's view briefly as he crossed before her. When she could see clearly again she saw Garm raising a sword in time to turn aside Daven's attack with ease. She wanted to stay, to help, but knew that she couldn't. She stood and ran for the tree line. She nearly made it.

Knocked from her feet by a violent shove, Kina heard the clash of swords above her. The two fighters separated, giving Kina opportunity to scramble on her hands and knees away from danger. Kina turned and looked as she noted Garm and Nadia facing off. It seemed that Garm had left Daven and Lyle behind in order to stop her, but Nadia had shoved her aside at the last moment.

Garm no longer seemed so at ease and looked as if he were preparing for the fight of his life. Nadia seemed as though she were enjoying herself and she stood relaxed with blade in hand and a grin on her face that Kina didn't much like.

"I did not realize you would answer to the likes of Gawthrain," Nadia's voice taunted.

"He serves my purpose for now," he responded, glancing at Kina briefly. She shied further back from him, but he didn't move. Nadia stepped between them.

"No, Garm. The time for games has passed. Now we find out whether or not your boasts are true. I may not have the strength of my sisters, but I am still enough to bring down the likes of you."

Garm's focus returned to Nadia, and he smirked with an odd grin that filled Kina with dread. "Then perhaps it is time to end this. You never did know what battles were worth fighting, did you?" And with a pulse of power that Kina could feel, Garm began to grow. Clothing ripped away as his skin rippled and darkened. Terrified, Kina stumbled back before gaining her feet and running for the safety of the trees. The sound of his laughter grew louder and deeper. She dared not look back until she reached the safety of the trees. Once she had though, she trembled at the sight she beheld. There were tales of such creatures, legends of how they had the power to walk among mankind in secret, but she never expected such truth in the myths. Nadia stood before a dragon, covered with large red scales so dark in color that they were nearly black. Her eyes were drawn to the big black wings that stretched out behind the creature. They flapped twice forcing a powerful wind down that blew at Kina's clothes and hair and nearly flung her to the ground. The trees bent as though caught in a hurricane. The dragon stood taller than most buildings that Kina had seen in her lifetime, easily half as tall as the Duke's castle. She wondered if the soldiers in the camp would attack or flee from such a creature before just as quickly wondering how they could ever be brave enough to stand against a dragon.

Kina jumped at the touch of a hand on her shoulder, nearly leaping out of her hiding spot in fright. Lyle steadied her, looking quite dazed himself.

"Come, we must go."

She only nodded and allowed herself to be pulled along before remembering that she alone knew where the entrance way was. Regaining her wits, she sped up so that she could lead Lyle in the correct direction.

In a distant part of the back of her mind she cursed herself for missing the battle that raged behind her. Witnessing a goddess taking arms against one of the greatest of magical creatures ever to breathe was something that she had never dared to hope for. This was the stuff of legends.

The sound and feel of a roar so powerful that it shook the earth, however, reminded Kina that this was real and unlike a story, there was the potential that she would not see her friends again. She looked over her shoulder to see the dragon spitting flames from its mouth at the ground, or more likely at somebody standing upon it. She hesitated, worrying for her friends, but Lyle grabbed her by the arm and dragged her forward once more. He was right, she realized. Nadia and Daven were doing their part, she had to do her part and take Lyle to the sword.

It didn't stop her glancing back as they ran, though.

Once more she laid eyes on the remains of the old temple ruin. This time she paused at a distance to look for dangers outside rather than within. The hole in the ground seemed wider now, probably trampled down by many feet since its rediscovery. The castle walls of Brighton were obvious from the tree line and she could see that the fires still raged out of control among the tents of the soldiers. Now it seemed that the battle was no longer being fought and the camps were deserted. The ring wall around Brighton was populated by soldiers at the ready, and she didn't need to guess the cause of their retreat. The ground was trembling still from the battle between Garm and Nadia, and now and then Kina caught a flash of light from the corner of her eye. The thunder she heard was more likely caused by their fighting than the still growing storm above.

Lyle pushed up against her, looking about warily. "So where is the cave?"

"There," she answered, pointing at the hole.

Lyle looked to her, his face looking concerned and slightly alarmed. "That is not what I call a cave," he remarked darkly. "I have seen freshly dug graves bigger than that hole."

Kina shivered. "It's bigger than it seems," she added. That seemed enough for Lyle and he pulled her forward once more. Lyle paused once more at the lip of the entrance way to give Kina an almost pleading look before climbing down into the darkness.

She climbed down after him and quickly surveyed her surroundings. Even though it was still light above, the storm clouds were making it darker than it appeared and once inside the collapsed temple much of that light was lost. Lyle would be blind within ten paces of where they stood. She spotted exactly what she had hoped. Several abandoned torches discarded by those who had looted the crypt as they reached the surface. She grabbed two and set to relighting one. Almost at once, the walls were illuminated as she brought the first torch back to life.

"Here," she said, handing it over to Lyle. "Keep behind me. There were traps down here." She wondered if there were any left to be tripped after the looting had finished. Would there be more bodies or would they have been pulled to the surface by comrades? Another question that she found herself not really interested in discovering the answer to.

"What about you?"

Kina hesitated before realizing that Lyle was unaware of her ability to see in the dark. It appeared as though Daven still had not told him everything about her. "I can see fine. Better without the torch blinding me." She began to move, slowly at first but she picked up speed as she traveled deeper within. "Step lightly. We'll be in the city before long."

Lyle fell into step behind her without complaint, though she could tell from the shadows on the wall that he held the torch like an amateur. He would be nearly blinded by the light of the flame, ruining whatever night vision he may have had.

"You should probably hold the torch up away from your eyes. You will see more and the ceiling here is still quite high." Almost at once her shadow slid lower on the floor as the torch was raised behind her. "Do they not teach soldiers this in Faneria?"

There was a hesitation that Kina predicted would have been filled by Lyle's gruff dismissal, but instead he answered her with what sounded like embarrassment.

"I must admit I have neglected certain duties. I have not had to deal with night watch."

"Why is that?" She brushed aside a series of roots and stood clear of the falling debris that the movement caused.

"Prestige and politics." The torch moved behind her as Lyle cleared the roots and avoided setting fire to them. "I think my commanders have feared repercussions for assigning such a task."

"Daven did mention your family name carried some weight."

"Some," Lyle admitted. "But I must continue to do the same tasks as others in my position would. We are not so different despite our standing."

"I suppose you have to do more now," Kina noted. She looked about, noting that the bodies of the fallen had indeed been dragged away from where they had died. She couldn't read the tracks in the ground, but she didn't need to. The bodies were gone.

"Now?" Lyle's question seemed curious and even slightly annoyed by her observation. "Why do you feel that to be so?"

Kina paused, and risked exposing her eyes to the flame by turning to face him. "Because of what Daven did. You had to volunteer to bring him back to prove that the family name would not influence your judgment."

Lyle's face remained solemn. "No, Kina. The family bond should not be broken. It is what the Hitchcliffe clan can call their own. I must do what is right, but I do so for the good of family. If it were duty alone I would not have volunteered. I may not agree with Daven's choices but I do not dismiss him."

Kina looked at Lyle strangely. "Why? I don't understand. He committed crimes against Faneria. Is this not a mark against your family name? I thought that was why you were so angry with him."

Lyle sighed. "It is complicated. Yes, his crimes look badly upon us. He is no more proud of those actions than I am."

"But, you said he stole from a Fanerian lord."

"Perhaps you should keep walking," Lyle told her, his tone not sounding overly annoyed by her questions but reminded her of the importance of her mission. She turned and carefully began to pick her way over the rough floor while she waited for her eyes to readjust to the darkness. "Daven is not a simple man. He is gifted with a sharp mind and able reflexes. He was once a scout with unequaled abilities and assured a position within the leadership of Faneria's armies due to his ability to think on his feet."

"What happened?"

"He tracked bandits one day back to a gypsy camp. When he returned to report to the Earl of Marrows, Fanerian soldiers were sent in and killed everybody. As far as nobility was concerned, the entire camp was feeding off the hard working people of the region and so needed to be removed. That included women and children. Daven was furious and retaliated. I do not know what he intended to do, but he made mistakes. The castle was damaged in his escape and his name was in ruin."

Kina thought again of what Nadia told her that night they shared alone. She had said that Daven was ruled by his emotions. It did seem to her that Daven was greatly concerned about her tale of the other children Drago had sent into the ruins to die before her. In fact, many of Daven's quirks made a little more sense. His dislike of those who followed orders, his disrespect for authority, it seemed to Kina that suddenly Daven didn't seem quite the mystery he had seemed before.

Whatever Daven's reasons for becoming a rogue, Kina found that she didn't care. He was who he was, and she was happy to have him with her.

Her return to the crypt was strangely quiet. It had been weeks since she was last here and yet in her mind it felt more recent. It had been completely looted of anything of value, and much of the writings on the walls had been marred by gouges in the rock itself. It seemed that those who had become wealthy from this place owed it little thankfulness. The old king had suffered one final injustice, his skull now smashed to pieces. She gave him a moment of silent prayer, much to Lyle's surprise.

"What is it you pray for here?"

"The fallen king," she responded. "When I discovered this place he lay peacefully resting. Drago's band destroyed this place and the remains."

"How do you know this was a king?" Lyle looked about curiously.

Kina looked at him and then surveyed the remains herself. "This may not look like much now, but there were treasures here when we arrived. The sword was entombed with him."

Lyle looked at her sharply before once more studying the ruined crypt more seriously himself. Kina abandoned her memories and returned to her task as the silence returned between them. She found the old tunnel that she had discovered before that led her to this crypt. It looked undisturbed, and she quickly made her way to it. She bit her lip and looked back to Lyle in slow realization of a new problem. She hadn't really thought through the fact that she had to squeeze through many sections of the tunnel herself. There was no possible way that Lyle would be able to fit through with her.

"Lyle," she began hesitantly, her mind whirling as she tried to find some alternative. "We have to find another way into Brighton."

There was alarm in his eyes as he turned to face her. "There is not time enough. What can I do to help?"

"You cannot help," she said softly. "The path is too narrow." She pointed at the opening in the wall despondently. Lyle looked at the collapsed passage in confusion. It was small certainly, but he could pass that far. She could see the trust and concern in his face as he met her eyes again and he didn't question her.

"Then you must go," he told her, his voice sounding thick with concern.

"No. I'll go with you. We'll find another way."

"Perhaps," Lyle agreed, "but perhaps not soon enough. You go, I will find another way."

"There are traps down here, and natural hazards. This place is not safe for the inexperienced."

"I will be cautious."

"What if I run into the Duke?" she asked, worrying now that she would have to stop the ceremony on her own.

"Kina, stop. I do not doubt your courage and neither should you. You must go."

Kina's mouth dropped open as she tried to argue the point further. She knew she was the only one to reach inside Brighton quickly now. She didn't want to leave Lyle alone in this place, but before she could give further voice to her concerns she picked up the sounds of somebody else inside the ruin. She motioned for Lyle to be silent and she turned to face the way they had come. Light flickered against the wall as a torch was brought closer and a darkly familiar laugh chilled Kina to the core.

"Drago," she whispered, startling Lyle beside her and his hand fell to the sword at his side.

"Go," he whispered back to her.

"No," she pleaded, shaking her head frantically.

"Go!" Lyle ordered, drawing his sword and taking a step forward.

Drago strolled around the corner, torch in one hand and sword in the other. The smile that he directed at Kina was not inviting. She took a step back unconsciously.

"I told you I would find you, Kina. I don't know how you created that diversion up there, but I commend you on your ingenuity." Drago grinned with dark pleasure. "Is that tiny hole how you found your way into this place?"

"Kina," Lyle growled, stepping between her and Drago abruptly.

Hesitantly, Kina took Lyle's warning. Without further words, Kina dove at the tunnel, sliding on her hands and knees on the dirty floor. She ignored the pains and began to crawl in as fast as she could.

"Don't you dare turn away from me! Kina!" Drago screamed after her. "Get of my way!" Behind her she could hear the scuffle of feet and the sound of metal on metal. Lyle could beat Drago, she thought with confidence. He could win, and then he would meet her inside the walls of Brighton.

Unfortunately, her fears were not so easily defeated.

Despite her concerns, Kina pushed herself forward. She had no need to stop in here. Without a torch she could still see well enough to pass through the darkness which would have blinded her before. Her ears could pick up every sound; the scurrying of something small as it escaped deeper within; the sound of the fight behind her.

She was able to travel quickly, now that she journeyed unencumbered by torch or bag. When she could stand once more, Kina moved at a pace hurried by need which bordered on reckless. She reached the collapsed floor and came to a stop once more. This place still drew her in uncertainly. It was a mystery that she didn't understand. How did the earth open up into a hole beneath the ruined temple in such a manner? There were no eroding waters here.

It was a mystery that Kina didn't have time to unravel now. If she survived this day, she would have to return to this place and answer this riddle. Kina made her way back to the ledge of stone to make her way to the other side.

Kina hesitated and looked deep into the darkness. Oddly, she noted that the hole was not so randomly made. While damaged where the stone floor had collapsed, down in the darkness she could see that the walls of the hole were smooth and unmarred. As Kina's eyes focused upon the hole she was greeted with greater detail. Deep below Kina noted that there was another tunnel connecting to the hole, another level to the ruined temple not yet explored. This one Kina reasoned would be untouched by any other since all other entrances had been destroyed so long ago.

They did not know with any certainty that the Duke was in Brighton. In fact, she recalled that her companions had agreed that the Duke would be attempting this summoning in secrecy. He was at the doorway to the Gods of Light, under the city. No, Nadia said it felt closer than the city just outside.

"Will I find the Duke if I follow this tunnel?" Kina asked the question, but she didn't expect an answer. Her mind was already weighing in facts and reasoning in her head as she tried to form her own conclusion. Perhaps it was time to find out why this hole called out to her. Kina cringed as she looked at the path she needed to take. If she missed her jump, she could fall much further to her death. She knew the floor was far enough that she would not survive. The gods did seem to be favoring her and this was not a task they wished her to fail in. She could not fail.

"Veran, please allow me to find my way. Many lives depend on my success and I've not the time to be lost. Guide my feet." She closed her eyes and took a deep calming breath. The goddess didn't answer and Kina never expected to hear a response, but she hoped that Veran would allow her to make the right decision and judgment.

Opening her eyes again, Kina focused on the entrance below. It had to be the right path. She couldn't define why she felt that way, but the calling deep within her seemed to be leading her down. Nodding to herself, Kina set her feet in the dirt and clenched her hands. Rope would have been nice, but she had not intended to explore new trails today. Kina ran forward the final steps to the lip and jumped. It felt as though she was floating for a moment, her arms flailing wildly as she covered half the distance over the hole. And then she felt herself begin to fall. With a shriek, she plunged downward. Her thoughts formed one distinct thought in her mind which she believed entirely; I'm dead.

The fall was short, however, as Kina's flailing hands grabbed the ledge. She hit the wall hard, forcing the air from her lungs loudly, but her grip remained strong. Gasping for air, she looked up into the new tunnel and readjusted her grip. Her legs hurt, her knees were scraped and she knew she was covered with bruises from the day's worth of action, but she was still alive. Kina climbed up, a tedious and tiring process, and sat panting alone on the floor of this dark tunnel, unable to turn back. She was on a new path now, and this one could have predated the temple ruin. These walls looked as though they had been cut from the rock itself, and polished to such a smooth surface that she doubted it could be natural. Could this be the path the Gods of Light walked when they came to this world? Kina began to walk it slowly, studying any scratch or loose pebble for signs of the past.

It took what seemed to Kina as an eternity of walking through the unchanging tunnel before she had sign of anything. There was a voice speaking ahead. She could hear the tones but not the words nor meaning. The voice echoed in the enclosed passages and the words were not spoken as though in conversation either, but in a steady staccato of chanting. Kina raised her hand to her chest, and stood still as she fought the belief that she had found the Duke. She had been lucky to the extreme if this was the case.

Kina moved slower through the tunnel now as she walked with greater caution. She put each foot down carefully so that she would make as little noise as possible. Light began to glow on the tunnel ceiling in the distance. To Kina, this indicated that there was another level below her and that her path would soon intersect. She guessed this was where the chanting was coming from and was not surprised that she was able to confirm this as she got closer. The tunnel came to a stop beyond the intersection;

her only option was down into the light. Kina crawled the final distance to peer over.

This was not just a tunnel she found, but a chamber of great size. The floor was lined with heavy white stone that reflected the light of the torches that hung on the walls. There was also an odd shimmering pool that looked like water, although it stood vertically against one wall. It moved and flowed like water yet stayed within the stone disk without pouring out onto the floor. It had to be magic of some kind, and Kina felt her gaze drawn into it.

Fighting the urge to study the pool, Kina refocused upon her task. Indeed the Duke was present. Slightly overweight, donning armor, cape and sword, Gawthrain leaned against the stone wall in wait for his plan to come to fruition. Facing the pool stood another cloaked figure, seemingly illuminated in oddly glowing mists that shifted about as he moved. This one did the chanting that Kina could hear, but still the words were meaningless to her. This was a mage, she realized, a real magic user. The mists she saw were similar to the dark symbols that surrounded Nadia, but were different too. In his hands he held an old book and at his feet lay Vashnir. There were no guards in the room, though Kina noted there were numerous smooth-walled passages from the chamber. She would have to use one of those passages to escape, as she doubted she could climb back up into this one, and even if she could she wouldn't be able to climb out of the pit at the other end of the tunnel.

Now that she had found the ceremony, she needed to disrupt it. She couldn't imagine how she would manage that. She could drop in and immediately attack the cloaked mage with the dagger she had received from Nadia, but she doubted she could escape the Duke. That would leave him with Vashnir and spell so that he could try again.

She could attack the Duke head-on, but she doubted that she

would survive long enough to even give pause to the mage.

Neither plan sounded all that plausible to Kina, but her options were limited. She chose the option she felt had the greatest chance of success and tensed her body. The mage had to be stopped. In the end, her life was worth the trade to prevent Nephrita from returning to this world under the control of any man. She breathed in deeply, trying to keep her hands from shaking any worse. She backed away from the hole slowly and stood ready to meet her destiny. She drew her dagger and held it tight.

With one last calming breath, Kina ran forward. She leapt down recklessly into danger, landing heavily behind the mage. Kina steadied herself almost immediately, surprising both herself at maintaining her balance and the Duke who looked at her with stunned disbelief. The mage barely had time to turn before she slashed at him with her knife. She missed, but the result was just as effective. He stumbled back over his long robe, dropping the book and falling down. The mists immediately raced away from his fallen form and dissipated into the air.

Kina wasted no time before collecting Vashnir in her free hand and turning to face a charging Gawthrain. Sword drawn and a look of hatred distorting his face, Kina barely had time to ready herself. Not that being ready made her any less vulnerable when Gawthrain swung his sword. Rather than attempting to fight, Kina stumbled out of his path as quickly as she could. She ducked low, barely avoiding his slashing attack. The sound of the sword whistled over her head as she tried to get her feet back beneath her.

There was an opening ahead of her now. All she needed to do was escape into the tunnel and then she would be gone. It might take her a while to find the surface, but she knew she could escape into the darkness and hide.

It only took one step. Kina heard the Duke grunt with effort to turn and attack and she was caught mid stride unable to react as the blade of his sword struck at her. A shriek tore from her throat as the sword slashed her left shoulder open, sending Nadia's dagger flying. Black ripples spread across the glowing waters of the pool marking spot the dagger had entered, but there had been no splash on impact or any other sign that an object had passed through. Kina fell to the ground and slid on the dusty floor. Vashnir remained in front of her, but with tears in her eyes it appeared blurry. Her arm wasn't too bad, if anything the sharp edge had only cut a gash as long as her finger into her shoulder. It did hurt though, and any movement she made sent new flashes of pain through her body. She forced herself to look away from her bloodied sleeve and focus on the Duke once more.

Gawthrain contented himself with gloating at her proudly beyond swords reach. The mage slowly stood behind him, looking unimpressed by her attempted heroics. Gawthrain shook his head.

"I do not know how you were able to avoid my scouts or how you have come to find me now, but I assure you that your luck changes here. Do not think that I will spare your life now you have brought yourself between me and the power fated to be mine."

Kina gritted her teeth, and gripped Vashnir as she got up on her knees. "And do not expect me to give up my life."

"You cannot defeat me, girl."

"No," she agreed. It didn't look like she would be rejoining the others. He and the mage both stood between her and any escape route. The mage, for his part, seemed content to let Gawthrain do the work, but she fully expected him to cast a spell should she get past the Duke.

At least the Duke's plans would be thwarted once and for all. Kina grinned as he allowed her time to catch her breath. He seemed happy enough just to watch her, oblivious to the new threat to his plan. "I can't defeat you in combat, Lord Gawthrain. I can, however, deny you your prize." If she couldn't escape, she could at least prevent further attempts at the spell by throwing the sword through the portal. Kina pushed herself into a run from her knees, driving forward toward the magic doorway, uncertain herself if she would throw herself into the strange pool with the sword. Instantly Gawthrain became aware of what she had planned and screamed out defiantly. No doubt he was slowly getting his body to speed as he tried to stop her. The mage called out as well, trying his best to instill fear within her that he would cast a spell upon her. It took precious moments to cast a spell, and Kina had a good head start.

Only paces from the magic doorway, Kina's eyes widened and she slid unsteadily to stop on the dusty stone floor. Whispering, scratchy voices that made her blood run cold. They sounded far off and yet coming closer, and they were coming from the other side of the gateway. Gawthrain tackled her into the ground heavily, though perhaps he was as much surprised by her sudden stop as he had failed to bring his weapon into position to finish her.

"You should not have stopped," he growled into her ear. It was not his voice she was listening to. She could still faintly hear the sounds that sapped away her strength. They were definitely getting closer.

"We must go," she whispered sharply. "If you want to live, we must go now!"

"I must do nothing you say," he returned, pulling on her hair sharply to snap her head back off the ground. She winced but didn't scream out. Instead she refocused her senses on the approaching danger.

"Listen," she panted out. "They smell blood. Wraiths!"

"Wraiths?" Gawthrain laughed out loud. He ripped Vashnir away from her grip and stepped back off her. Kina quickly rolled over so that she could face the living threat without putting her back to the pool. "You expect me to believe in legends?"

The mage no longer looked as confident as the Duke sounded. He looked warily around the chamber, clearly rattled by the thoughts of wraiths. The mage would know the truth of her words, and apparently he had a healthy respect for the threat they posed.

"We must go," Kina insisted. "Can't you hear them?"

"My Lord," the mage spoke in a soft whispering voice that sounded shaken. "We should do as she says."

"No," Gawthrain remarked, looking at his mage without further concern. "We will finish the ceremony."

"We can return," the mage argued, as he stepped back away from the gateway. Kina herself was feeling more ill at ease the louder the whispers got. She raised herself slowly while watching Gawthrain's weapons for any sign of attack. The Duke let her stand, holding out Nephrita's sword to the mage expectantly.

Kina caught the stare of the elderly mage and she shared an understanding with the magic user that crossed boundaries. It was time to leave this place. The old man turned quickly with his robes swishing around his body and ran down one of the tunnels out of the chamber. The suddenness of his departure startled the Duke who scolded the mage loudly from where he stood. Kina backed away from both Duke and doorway as she reevaluated her own chances. The ceremony was broken this day, but she had not removed any of the pieces necessary for him to try again. He held Vashnir, but the book that the mage had read from lay on the stone floor. She didn't like the trade, but it was all she could reach.

It was then she noted the movement in the shadows. The wraiths were already around them. She looked about quickly, spotting several surrounding them in the chamber. Fear peaked and then seemed to fade as Kina looked at the suddenly shaken

Duke of Deverell. So her quest had come to an end. At least she would see the fall of the evil lord who had started it all.

"What is this?" Gawthrain demanded, turning around with hopes of finding an opponent he knew how to fight. Kina wondered if he knew the danger he was in. "Face me now!"

"You will die here," she told him with a calm voice that surprised even her. "We die together. The commoner and the noble, buried forever in this forgotten place."

"No," Gawthrain declared loudly. He charged head long at one of the shadows, raising Vashnir high above him. "Fight me!"

Kina's breath caught in her throat, realizing that she would survive long enough to witness one more death. Her mind began to move faster as she fought the impulse to give in. If she was going to die, she was going to die trying to break free of this trap. Kina charged forward, grabbing the spell book on the run, and headed for the nearest tunnel. Behind her she could hear Gawthrain still yelling out his challenge to the wraiths. And then she could hear him screaming. She turned to witness the Duke being enveloped by the formless shadows as they attacked from all sides. Blood splattered as armor and skin were split. His legs lacked the protection of plate armor and were showing signs of being slashed repeatedly. The wounds were not fatal, at least not yet. Gawthrain turned and flailed wildly at his attackers, as Kina backed away. He caught one of the wraiths with the sword and it passed clean through as she had expected.

Light flared through the chamber, casting down the shadows and darkness with a white glow that burned her eyes. Kina's skin prickled and her hair filled with static as the wave passed over her. The sound of the Duke's screams were silent as was the whispering of the wraiths. They hadn't faded, they had simply stopped. Kina looked about in this new bright world of white, confused and wary of new dangers. She heard nothing to suggest a need to worry, and just as abruptly, the light disappeared. The wraiths that had stood before her were gone. The Duke could be heard rasping on the floor, but otherwise the room was silent once more.

Kina turned about, looking for the wraiths in confusion. They never abandoned a kill like this. They always finished what they started. Yet the Duke lay on the floor still alive. True he was grasping at terrible wounds to his leg and was panting hard, but he was still living. He was cut in other places as well, claw marks that ran deep into the flesh of his arms and even through the armor of his chest. The wild look in his eyes suggested he was in great pain, but was still aware enough to pose a danger to her should she let her guard down.

"Come to," he panted uncomfortably and he licked his dry lips before continuing, "gloat?"

"Hardly," she responded. She looked around again, but still did not see the source of the power that had dispatched the wraiths. She would ask Gawthrain, but she knew he would not know. Instead she focused on his wounds. "Do you need help?"

"You would not," he answered darkly, "help me."

"I would," she answered firmly. It was the truth, though only because she needed him almost as much as he needed her. She didn't know how to escape from these tunnels, and while she might find her own way, it would take time. "Those cuts are deep and I doubt you could walk more than five strides on that leg. I hold you no grudge, though my companions might. I can help you travel back to your city or send help to retrieve you."

The Duke looked at her suspiciously. "And why would," he again paused for a breath, "you do that?"

Kina smiled, though she thought later that it may have appeared less than friendly at that moment. "I will take back Vashnir as price. A fair deal for sparing your life, would you not agree?"

The Duke pulled the sword closer to himself, looking to her

warily. Kina waited, knowing Gawthrain would have to come to the conclusion that he would require her help. It wasn't a long wait. He tried to throw the weapon at her, but with so little strength that it barely left his grip before clattering on the stone floor. "Fine."

Kina looked at the Duke and considered the weight of his bulk and armor. "We'll need to leave your armor behind, Lord Gawthrain. And any other weapons you carry."

Again he looked as though he was going to protest but relented again and silently pulled his own sword from his scabbard and discarded it on the floor. Kina approached slowly, retrieving Vashnir from the floor gently. She gazed at it almost fondly as she recalled how much trouble it had been to her, and yet she had come back to retrieve it. She hesitated, noting one small change to the sword. The crystal that she had placed into the hilt had cracked. Fractures ran through its length over and over again, but the stone had not shattered or fallen out. When that had happened, she didn't know.

"Do not make me wait," the Duke growled from the floor. "I cannot remove my armor without help."

Kina sighed, and slid Vashnir away at her side. She stashed the spell book into the largest of her belt pouches, though she was unable to close it and she felt a few stitches burst at the effort to make it fit. Her hands free, she looked to the Duke and considered whether or not helping his bleeding body from this place was the ugliest of tasks she had yet to perform in life.

"I hope you know a shorter path out of this place," Kina grumbled as she set to work.

Chapter Nine

It was nightfall when Kina returned to the fields outside the walls of Brighton. It had taken longer to carry Gawthrain's weight through the tunnels than she had hoped, made longer by the pains of her own injuries. She worried that her companions had long left her behind and was anxious to rejoin them. The sky had cleared and whatever storm had come passed away long before. She limped past numerous abandoned weapons and ruined tents, ignoring the wary looks she received from the soldiers who solemnly cleaned up the signs of battle. She could imagine what they thought they saw in her now. The monster they had chased from these walls before now walked past them easily, armed and bloodstained from battle, but clearly victorious. She felt powerful.

She had returned the Duke to his city, but had left him once they had reached open air once more. He had enough supporters to help him further and she would do best by retreating before he decided to cancel their deal. She expected him to do so and she didn't hold any grudge for it. He was a noble lord, he had his image to maintain. So far, if he had ordered her capture, it seemed that his orders were slow to be passed through the ranks. None of the soldiers she passed had fight left after the events of today.

Kina returned to the place in the fields where Daven and Nadia battled the dragon named Garm. There were signs of fighting here as well, but she saw little sign of her companions. The dragon too was gone. Left behind were huge portions of scorched grass and deep holes ripped into the ground. Had she stayed in the city she could have asked who had been the eventual victor, but Kina no longer expected any other outcome. If she had been able to stop the ceremony, then Nadia and Daven would have seen to Garm's defeat. She did worry, however, when she did not see them waiting for her.

She retraced her steps back to the cave, hopeful that perhaps her companions waited for her return from the ruin below. So she traveled in the darkness, calling out their names in hopes that she would be reunited. None answered her. By the time she reached the tree line she was running as best as she could and her throat was aching. It was much to her relief when she finally saw another living being at the entranceway.

"Lyle!" she cried out, instantly recognizing his form sitting next to the cave. His head jerked up immediately, and he rose the moment his eyes could pick her out of the darkness. She could see the relief in his features, and the disbelief that she appeared before him. There was more that Kina could see hidden in his expression. He must have defeated Drago, but his eyes seemed different to her now. In truth she didn't care, she was just relieved to see him again. She raced forward and embraced him, much to his surprise. Reluctantly he patted her shoulders. She winced at the pain it caused to her wound, but restrained the urge to flinch back.

"I had nearly given up hope," he told her.

"I couldn't return through the same path," she said apologetically. "I'm sorry to cause you worry."

"Nadia said you must have failed."

Kina pushed back off Lyle, and looked into his eyes. "But I stopped it," Kina answered. She drew Vashnir part way so that he could see for himself. "See? And I have the spell book. I interrupted the summoning ceremony. Gawthrain can't attempt it again."

Lyle too looked confused. "But Nadia said she felt the power of the spell."

"The mage was still chanting when I stopped them. He didn't finish."

"Nadia did say it was different this time," Lyle acknowledged. He looked skyward as if further troubled by the insight Kina had provided. "Something was released this day."

"Perhaps Nadia felt only the power of the spell being released without completion?"

"I do not know. Magic is an uncertain power, even to those who seek to control it." Kina thought back to the odd light in the chamber which had dispersed the wraiths. Had that been the power that Nadia had felt? Kina could think of no other magic that could have taken place. She shuddered.

Lyle studied her and shook his head, once again a faint smile on his lips that seemed to ease his spirits.

"You look a mess. How you could have defeated the likes of…" His voice trailed off as he regarded her with greater focus. He seemed to strain his vision in the light of the stars to see with greater detail, and Kina suddenly felt uncomfortable under his scrutiny. "Turn around," he ordered, though his voice was not unfriendly. She paused a moment, not sure what it could be to cause a change in her friend's mood, but she did as she was told. She turned in a slow circle before facing him once more.

A smile slowly reached the corners of his mouth. "You changed back," he told her.

Wordlessly, Kina felt at her head with her hands. The ears were gone. She had her own ears back! She looked over her shoulder immediately, and noted that indeed the tail too was gone. The surge of emotion inside her nearly made her leap in the air. She very nearly embraced Lyle a second time, but restrained herself at the last moment with a blush. She didn't care how it happened, or why she hadn't noticed, but she was grateful to have her own features back. She considered momentarily the fact that she could still see through the darkness so clearly and how she seemed to be aware of the sounds of the forest still. Not everything was back the way it was.

"I assume you were unaware," Lyle noted. "I am glad for you."

"After so long, I doubted I'd ever be free of it." She didn't understand magic any more than Lyle or Daven so she wondered if she would ever know exactly what it was that did this to her. She also found that at this moment she didn't much care about the cause. "This is wonderful!"

"So we did accomplish what we had set out to do." He looked skyward, looking a bit more relieved.

"Where are the others?"

"Nadia continues to pursue Garm. I fear she will not relent now until one of them is destroyed." He sounded saddened by the thought. She couldn't imagine why Nadia would take such a dark and solitary path. Kina understood the betrayal, and the battle, but a determined path of vengeance was incomprehensible to her. But then, Kina thought sadly, Nadia had lived a much different and secretive life. Her reasons would not be so plain to see.

"I plan to return to my post. You are welcome to join me if you still wish my training you."

Kina considered the invitation briefly. "Perhaps, someday. There is much I would like to see now, and the need to fight seems to have diminished."

"Good."

"And Daven, do you plan to take him back with you?"

"Daven is free now," Lyle remarked, looking away from her. "He fell to the dragon." Kina stared at Lyle in disbelief. Her legs felt suddenly weakened and she stumbled back before steadying herself. "Daven would have preferred it this way. He gave you your chance to reclaim your life, and he escapes the reach of the Guard. He gets to look like the hero. In a way, he can reclaim some of his honor through his actions." It was strange to her how calm Lyle seemed when he spoke of his brother's death.

"How could you?" Kina whispered, though even she was unsure whether she cursed Lyle for his coldness or Daven for dying. She directed her anger at Lyle, uncertain of even why she was angry. "How can you so calmly talk of the death of your brother while his killer goes free?"

"A dragon is outside any vengeance I can bring." Lyle's frustration and anger could be heard openly for the first time that Kina could remember. "Nadia already seeks the head of Garm, so what more does my sword offer? I must accept reality and move on, as should you."

She could not think of a rebuttal no matter how hard she wanted to. Her emotions demanded that she do something more, but her mind worked against her.

"Daven should never have been involved. I asked him to help me, and made myself sound so helpless. How is this fair?"

"He did what he wanted, and you can take no blame in that." Lyle slumped. "Kina, we all knew the risks involved. That any of us survived this day is no small miracle. Be strong."

"I can't," she said with a sniffle.

"The future will tell if that is true." Lyle gathered up his slightly larger bag of belongings, letting her cry herself out in silence. She watched him, but she didn't know what more to say or do. How could her happiest day suddenly come crashing down so?

Her mind cursed her with memories of Daven, a lopsided grin on his face as he teased her. It was a trait that he had not favored her with since she had caught him with Nadia, but it was the expression she remembered most favorably. She remembered how he seemed at ease with her, despite all that she appeared. She remembered how he had taken it upon himself to lead a frightened girl through a foreign land to find a cure. He had helped her one last time this day, allowing her to escape with Lyle into the ruin.

Lyle's tasks seemed unhurried, as though he were merely keeping busy. Now that her tears had run dry, he tossed the pack over his back, and glanced her way. It was clear that he no longer planned to stay the night in the proximity of this place. There was pain in his expression, the pain of losing the brother he had journeyed to save.

She was wrong to accuse him of being uncaring, he hurt with a pain far closer to the heart than she did.

"You said there were things you wanted to see, girl." He fixed her with a hard stare that she found nearly returned her to tears. She would be strong, for his sake. "Perhaps it is time to move on and seek them out."

She could only nod. She dried her eyes with the back of her hands and tried to swallow the lump that ached within her throat. Lyle was already walking away, leaving her alone by the entrance to the ruin. She had missed some subtle clue, and now he too seemed intent on leaving her.

"Lyle, wait," she said, her voice sounding rough. She tried to smile when he turned to face her, and while she could only manage a brief and very forced expression, she had little doubt that Lyle missed the attempt. "Could I join you? At least for a little while? I don't have any money left, but I can help you carry some of the load. I also have a book that should be in the hands of somebody who could better protect it than I."

Lyle looked as though he were considering her request before he nodded. "If you also tell me how you came to possess this book, I will accept your company."

"My shoulder still hurts, so not too much weight."

"Why is your shoulder sore?" His tone sounded as though his

patience was strained, but his expression never hinted towards displeasure.

"The Duke cut me with his sword," she responded in answer as she jogged to his side.

"I hope you cut him right back," Lyle gruffly answered. She didn't see a smile, but she wondered if it was there the same. Perhaps he even enjoyed her company to some extent.

"This better be quite the story, you seem to be doing very little carrying."

"I'm carrying the book," she reminded him with forced cheeriness.

"I should sell you for a horse."

9 780986 649325